"Will you miss me while I'm gone?" Matt asked, taking her hand.

Jennifer searched his face with a thoroughness he found disconcerting. "It's madness, you know. The way you make me feel every time you touch me . . . or look at me." She raised a hand to his face and traced the line of his eyebrows with a delicacy he found wildly erotic.

He took a deep breath and battled for control. He wasn't a teenager, and he wasn't going to act like one. He was a man who desired her, and he was going to teach her how exciting that desire could be. Hot, thorough, satisfying desire.

"How do I make you feel, Jenny?" He brought her other hand to his chest so she could feel his heart beating. "Can you tell me? Or would you rather listen to me tell yo ı what you do to me, what fantasies I want to share with you?"

"Tell me," she whispered. . . .

WHAT ARE *LOVESWEPT* ROMANCES?

They are stories of true romance and touching emotion. We believe those two very important ingredients are constants in our highly sensual and very believable stories in the *LOVESWEPT* line. Our goal is to give you, the reader, stories of consistently high quality that may sometimes make you laugh, sometimes make you cry, but are always fresh and creative and contain many delightful surprises within their pages.

Most romance fans read an enormous number of books. Those they truly love, they keep. Others may be traded with friends and soon forgotten. We hope that each *LOVESWEPT* romance will be a treasure—a "keeper." We will always try to publish

LOVE STORIES YOU'LL NEVER FORGET
BY AUTHORS YOU'LL ALWAYS REMEMBER

The Editors

Loveswept 601

Victoria Leigh
Flyboy

BANTAM BOOKS

NEW YORK · TORONTO · LONDON · SYDNEY · AUCKLAND

FLYBOY

A Bantam Book / March 1993

If you would be interested in receiving protective vinyl
covers for your Loveswept books, please write to this address
for information:

Loveswept
Bantam Books
P.O. Box 985
Hicksville, NY 11802

ISBN 0-553-44368-2

Published simultaneously in the United States and Canada

PRINTED IN THE UNITED STATES OF AMERICA

OPM   0 9 8 7 6 5 4 3 2 1

*For my husband, who showed me my wings,
then taught me to fly.*

One

The clouds outside the cockpit turned stark white. The C-141 Starlifter shuddered like a wet retriever exiting a lake that was just on the fluid side of freezing. Forked tongues of purple St. Elmo's fire danced on the bolts framing the windscreen—a moderately rare display of nature's terrifying beauty that failed to attract the attention of the men inside.

Matt Cooper, the aircraft commander, gripped the yoke tighter. "Copilot. Give me better intensity on the radar."

Rick Sturm, a young captain with whom Matt had been flying for the past three weeks, reached across the console to adjust the weather radar and scowled. "We're painting solid red straight ahead in the fifty-mile range. Thunderstorms everywhere."

"Lucky for us we don't have to go fifty miles." Matt's scowl matched his copilot's as he glanced at the interwoven blobs of red on the screen before returning his attention to the other instruments. They'd been relying solely on those instruments for the last twenty minutes, thanks to the typhoon-generated weather that blinded them to almost everything outside the cockpit.

The way things were going, they'd be landing blind too. Matt shrugged his shoulders in an attempt to ease the tension that had settled there when he wasn't paying attention. It wasn't a big deal. Instrument approaches were practiced and executed all the time as a matter of training and necessity. Landing in the path of a fast-approaching typhoon was also something he'd done before. Nearly twenty years of flying for MAC—Military Airlift Command, the section of the air force responsible for moving people and things around the world—had generated numerous flights around the Pacific when the weather was lousy and the mission was humanitarian.

No, air-evacuation flights weren't uncommon in the typhoon season, but they were cutting it close on this one. Typhoon Harry had changed course just hours earlier, turning at the same time from a playful spring fracas into a full-fledged rampage that had already leveled parts of several unoccupied islands due west of where they were heading.

Pilau, a tiny island paradise in the Pacific, was ten miles dead ahead of the Starlifter and in Typhoon Harry's direct path. Matt's orders were to evacuate whoever wanted to leave this American protectorate and take them to the nearest sanctuary until Harry blew itself out. He wouldn't worry about where they were headed until they'd landed, loaded up, and were back in the air.

If they managed to land at all. At the moment, winds were reported both in and out of limits, and landing in such conditions was definitely a judgment call. At Matt's request, the control tower that watched over the small landing strip had begun to report the winds and other pertinent information at two-minute intervals. The tower had also passed along the information that there were about forty civilians waiting in the terminal. The rest of the population had elected to wait it out.

Matt's fingers tightened even more around the yoke as he calculated just how far he could push the aircraft. He knew the aircraft's limits, and he knew his own. In emergency situations such as this, he often had to take chances that were normally

frowned upon. And it wasn't only landing that he had
to think about. If the winds whipped up in the short
time they were on the ground, there was a very real
chance they wouldn't be able to take off again—no
matter how far he was willing to stretch regulations.
If they were grounded by the typhoon, he would have
put his crew into a dangerous situation with only
hope and prayers to keep them safe.

Matt had the option of deciding the situation was
too dangerous to attempt any kind of evacuation. In
that case, they would simply turn tail, climb to an
altitude that even Harry couldn't reach, and fly back
toward blue skies and calm waters.

Matt wasn't one for giving up on a mission,
though. The control tower passed the news that
winds were holding within limits, and Matt took that
as an invitation. "Tell tower we're coming in."

Rick flashed Matt a grin and complied. "Tower,
this is MAC 60258 on final approach."

Matt kept the hand holding his flashlight clamped
on top of his blue flight cap to keep Harry from
tearing it off, leaving his other hand free to prod and
check the miscellaneous connections inside the
Starlifter's wheel well. Not good enough. He couldn't
see a bloody thing. The winds whipped his curse
across the tarmac as he stuffed the blasted hat into
the shin-level pocket of his flight suit. Pushing back
his straight blond hair, he switched on the flashlight
and resumed his preflight check. That was better. At
least he could see what he was supposed to be
looking at.

Satisfied, he ducked out of the wheel well and
made his way toward the aircraft's nose. The sky was
full of dark, roiling clouds, making it feel more like
dusk than the middle of the afternoon. About a
hundred yards down the runway, he could see tall
palms swaying in the wind, their enormous trunks
flexing as the tentacles of Typhoon Harry reached
out and taunted them.

The sooner they were out of there, the better.
Harry looked like he was about to get serious. Land-

ing hadn't been a picnic and takeoff was looking less and less attractive.

They had to hurry.

He was starting to sweat now, and Matt was pretty sure it was due to as much to his mounting urgency as to the brown leather jacket he wore over his green Nomex flight suit. The jacket was definitely overkill in this tropical climate, even in January, but would be essential once they were airborne and the aircraft cooled. For now, though, he'd just have to put up with it.

He made the routine checks in the forward wheel well, then looked up to see a bus arriving. They'd parked the aircraft out in the middle of nowhere, nearly a quarter mile away from the terminal, to avoid wasting the time it would take to taxi any closer. The passengers were being brought to them, and none too soon. He checked his watch and gave a satisfied grunt. It was going like clockwork. They'd be off Pilau in minutes.

As long as nothing went wrong—and a multitude of things could go wrong. Besides the winds. Things like annunciator lights that lit up when they weren't supposed to, or just the opposite. Things like oil leaks and flat tires. Although every member of his crew was a dedicated professional, Matt knew from years of experience that he needed to coordinate all their disparate activities. Sometimes, having another opinion or an extra pair of hands at the right moment saved five minutes when those minutes were critical. That was why he was outside now, helping the scanner—the second flight engineer—visually check what was necessary for a safe takeoff. He'd left it to the copilot and engineer to preflight the aircraft from the cockpit.

Matt left the forward wheel well and walked along the belly of the ungainly aircraft. The scanner—a young, enthusiastic man fresh out of the noncommissioned officers academy—had the side cowling up on engine number three.

"We used almost two quarts of oil on number three on the way out here, boss."

"Sounds excessive," Matt said, ducking beneath the engine to join him.

"It is, but . . ." The younger man shrugged and stared at the engine.

Matt finished for him. "But not excessive enough to keep us here, right?"

The scanner nodded. "That's right, boss."

Matt grinned and clapped him on the shoulder before moving away. No one wanted to stay on Pilau any longer than they had to. The winds were getting stronger.

Five minutes later, Matt rounded the tail of the C-141 and was headed back to the flight deck when he saw the door was barred by Chief Espinoza—the aircraft's loadmaster—and a redheaded woman with a small, wriggling child in each arm and an enormous caryall slung across her shoulder. They were arguing—the woman and the load, not the kids. Although Matt couldn't help but notice one of the children's high-pitched screams as they struggled for freedom.

The woman was pretty, he thought as he strode toward her. Not gorgeous, yet she had the kind of face that kept a man's interest once the more immediate fascinations of sex and mutual attraction had faded. She was wearing a sleeveless cotton T-shirt that hugged her small but nicely rounded breasts and was tucked haphazardly into a long, full skirt. Matt guessed the skirt was supposed to end around her knees, but it was presently bunching upward as she struggled to hold the kids against her. He was almost close enough to hear what the argument was about, when she hitched each child higher on her hips and turned away from the aircraft.

It looked as though she was headed back toward the terminal, on foot because the bus had already scuttled back toward shelter. Matt shot Load a puzzled look and went to intercept her. Load did likewise, circling from the other side until both men were blocking her path.

At closer survey, Matt judged her to be in her early twenties and the children about two, give or take a year. He didn't know much about kids.

He knew a little about women, though, and this one was going to be a handful. He could tell by the green eyes that flashed out at him from under an unruly mop of shoulder-length red hair. Her hair was glorious, dark red with rich brandy tones, but it was her eyes that held his attention. Expressive eyes, he thought. Easy to read. Easy to understand.

Those eyes all but spat bullets at Load and him as they looked down at her. Of course, they couldn't help but look down. Matt calculated from a superior height of nearly six feet that she couldn't have been more than five feet tall. He couldn't tell for certain, because the kids were squirming and she had to hunch over to keep them from jumping ship.

Considering she couldn't possibly weigh more than a hundred pounds dripping wet, he couldn't help but admire how she managed to keep from dropping either or both of them.

"I just have to run over to the terminal. I'll be right back," she yelled. One of the children—the one who was screaming—landed a punch in the vicinity of her breast. She gasped and hitched tot number one—a girl—upwards, away from such a tempting target.

Matt checked his grin and wondered if the red-headed mother knew her skirt was following the same path as the child.

He figured that if she knew, she was past caring. The child's howling was enough to overwhelm anyone's modesty.

The woman had terrific legs, he thought as the winds whipped what was left of her skirt above her thighs. About the only good deed Harry had done all day, Matt mused, clenching his jaw again to hold back his grin. As the woman tried to figure out how she was supposed to establish any degree of propriety with her arms already full of trouble, Harry took pity on her, blowing the skirt flat against her thighs.

Load ignored Harry's antics. "I told you once, ma'am," he shouted over the wailing wind and child. "We don't have the time for you to go back." He shot a glance at Matt, who knew the loadmaster didn't require confirmation from anyone. But as long as the aircraft commander was handy . . .

Matt nodded briskly. "He's right, ma'am. We're taking off in a couple of minutes. If you'll just get aboard—"

"I told him three times already," the woman interrupted, switching her frustrated scowl to Matt. "I can't do that until I get Carrie's doll. She must have dropped it in the terminal."

Matt's attention was momentarily diverted by the sound of her voice. It was a husky rasp that could either mean she had a cold or just naturally spoke like that. He found it sexy and hoped it was a permanent condition.

He eyed the two kids then and pushed aside all thoughts of sexy. This woman was married and he wasn't supposed to think about her that way. Even so, there was something about her that made him wish he'd met her first. . . .

Load was shaking his head. "And like I told you, ma'am, we don't have time for nonsense like that. Either you get on the aircraft this instant or you stay here and take your chances with the typhoon."

"This is about a doll?" Matt lifted a single brow and leveled a surprised stare on the load. This was his efficient and experienced loadmaster? Load just shrugged and raised his own eyebrows as if seeking divine intervention. He, too, was apparently off balance by the ridiculous argument.

In the normal course of events, they didn't argue with the cargo. Which was why, Matt mused, crew members almost universally preferred tanks and crates to people. They didn't talk back. They didn't cry, either. He shut his eyes in momentary frustration and wished he could shut his ears. Even over the typhoon, the noise the child was making was deafening.

The woman tossed her head in an attempt to get wisps of hair out of her eyes. "If you'll just get out of the way, I can get to the terminal and be back before you close the hatch."

"We call it a door," Matt said. "And Load's right. We don't have time."

"You don't understand—" she began.

His words sliced across hers. "You're right. I don't understand. I don't have time to understand." Matt could be stubborn if he chose. He chose. Not only that, he was getting angry. His forehead scrunched into a frown.

The guys back at the squadron would howl with laughter if they could see him now. He was best known for his unflappable, easygoing style of command. Nothing and no one ever got him mad, not really.

This redheaded pixie was cruising in uncharted waters.

Clearly oblivious to his warning signals, she glared at him, dire warnings of her own flaring in her eyes. "If I don't get Carrie's doll," she said evenly, "she'll scream nonstop to wherever we're going."

Tot number two—a boy, Matt decided—reached up and grabbed a handful of red hair. The woman didn't flinch except to settle the boy more firmly against her hip.

Matt cleared his throat and spared a glance at his watch. They were out of time. He leveled his very best commander's gaze on her and said, "I don't care if she screams for the next week."

He watched as her gaze flickered across the pilot's wings on his chest and up to his shoulders, where the silver oakleaf proclaimed his rank of lieutenant colonel. He saw the understanding register in her expression when her gaze returned to his. He was in charge of this show and she would just have to give in or go away.

She didn't do either.

"Of course you don't care," she said, wincing as tot number two grabbed another handful of hair. "You're going to be up front with things over your ears that prevent you from hearing anything you don't want to hear—screams and all."

She was right, but Matt wasn't about to admit it. He nodded to the load, then reached forward and plucked tot number one out of her arms before the woman knew what was happening. He handed the screaming child to the load, then reached for the other. The redhead would have had a chance of keeping that one were it not for timing: Tot number two chose that moment to dive backward with a fistful of hair in each of his chubby paws. Matt caught him before he could scalp his mother and held the child as she pried his fingers from her hair. The moment she was free, he gave the child to the load, who scrambled with them into the aircraft.

Before the woman could gear up for another argument, Matt plucked her carryall from her shoulder and looped it over his own. Then he scooped her into his arms and followed the load up the short flight of steps. She struggled and yelled, but there simply wasn't any future in it.

He was bigger and stronger. More important, he was determined to get his way. Maybe she didn't realize the danger they were in, but Matt was perfectly aware of it. Typhoon Harry didn't care about dolls any more than Load did.

She quit her struggles and arguments at the same time, but the noise level didn't recede. He could hear both of the children screaming, and he could only hope it wouldn't drive the rest of the passengers back out into the encroaching typhoon. Eager crew members pulled the door closed as he crossed it with the woman in his arms. He saw that Load had put the children into seats and was tucking blankets around them prior to buckling their belts. Matt plunked his own burden into the seat between the children, then retreated toward the front of the aircraft. Dual

screams followed him, but he wasn't overly bothered.

Problem solved.

Flinging himself up the ladder to the flight deck, he
scrambled into his seat and pulled on the head-
phones.

Peace at last.

Two

"MAC 60258. Winds 210 at 25 gust 40. Cleared for takeoff."

Matt listened to the detached, imperturbable voice of the tower controller and wished the winds were as calm. "Engineer, how close are we?"

"Crosswinds ten knots out of limits." The sergeant at the panel tapped his finger against a dial just in case it was stuck. It wasn't. He glanced over his shoulder. "Oil pressure on number three is holding."

Matt was glad that at least half the news was good. "Copilot. Inform the tower the winds they called are ten knots too strong." Occasionally, the tower exaggerated on the side of caution when relaying this vital information. And sometimes it was a difference of precisely when the controller checked his readings. Matt was simply asking the controller to look again . . . and find a better answer. He waited impatiently as the copilot made the relay.

Almost immediately, the radio crackled with the tower's response. "MAC 60258. We just had a new reading. Winds are 20 gust to 28."

Bingo. Matt flexed his fingers around the throttle and began takeoff sequence. Moments later, the heavy plane was speeding down the runway. The first drops of rain splattered against the Perspex windshield as Typhoon Harry all but tripped over itself in its hurry to

reach Pilau. The cockpit crew ignored Harry and concentrated on the job of getting the giant aircraft into
the sky.

It worked.

Matt felt the ground fall away beneath them. "Gear
up."

Rick Sturm pressed a button. A thud, and the
massive tires tucked into the belly of the Starlifter.

"Flaps up." Matt was almost smiling now. Another
few minutes and they'd be above Harry. Safe.

They were in the clouds, flying blind once again,
the winds buffeting the aircraft in such a manner as
to make the uninitiated wonder if they might have
been better off taking their chances down below.
Matt knew better.

The radio squawked. It was the control tower.
"MAC 60258 cleared to enroute frequencies. Good
luck."

Matt touched the dial of his radio and signaled
back, a job that was usually left to the copilot but
which he wanted to do himself this time. "Good luck
to you too," he said smoothly. "And thanks."

"Not to worry, Starlifter," tower said. "I've got a
hole just waiting for me to climb into."

Matt shared a grin with the copilot. "Then I sug-
gest you get going before Harry knocks you out of
that tower. MAC 60258, over and out."

Typhoon Harry was roaring in from the west, so
Matt headed in the opposite direction and started
thinking about where to go. Rick radioed ahead and
discovered that Guam was Harry's next probable
target. Too bad, Matt thought. Guam would have
been a short two-to-three-hour flight. Now they'd
have to go to Wake Island, about six-plus hours east
and north.

He wondered if tot number one's lungs would last
the entire trip.

Evidently, the child was going to make her very
best effort.

Chief Espinoza's voice came over Matt's radio headset. "Boss, you've got to do something about that kid. The rest of the passengers are threatening to tie a blanket around her head."

Matt glanced back, seeing that the load had climbed up into the cockpit. "Can't her mother do anything?"

Load shook his head. "It's not like she's not trying, sir. But without that blasted doll, there doesn't seem to be much anyone can do."

"Have you tried earplugs?" Another of the C-141's bows to utility was the lack of airline-quality sound control. Engine noise inside the aircraft was generally regarded as nearly intolerable—an exaggeration, but not entirely without foundation. For that reason, all passengers were routinely issued earplugs.

"Passed them out before we took off. They don't seem to be as effective against a kid's screams as they are against engine noise."

Matt could believe it. Something about a child's cries penetrated where other noises were suitably muted. It wasn't the kid's fault, he knew. The excitement of fleeing the typhoon added to the missing doll was likely more trauma than she could handle. Still, a crying child wasn't the best thing for nerves already stressed by Typhoon Harry.

On top of that, this was probably most of the passengers' first ride in a no-nonsense cargo plane. Earplugs were only one of the necessary adjustments. Blankets were equally essential. Even in the tropics, a cruising altitude of thirty-plus thousand feet tended to bring temperatures down to a point somewhat under "cool."

The military offered no apologies. The aircraft had never claimed to be anything more than a workhorse for the air force. Such things as adequate climate control, in-flight movies, and seats that faced forward had simply never been considered by those who designed the aircraft and its mission. Tanks or pallets of supplies, munitions and household goods didn't care if the perks of commercial travel were available or not.

Matt checked his watch. They were just one hour into the six-hour flight. Another five hours of listening to a child scream might be more than his passengers could stand. The last thing he needed was a lynching.

"Could you pass out the box lunches now?" he asked. "Maybe with some food in her stomach, she'll go to sleep."

"Already tried that, boss. She hit a guy on the head with her apple."

Matt turned in his chair to look at the load again. "Just how far did she throw it?"

"About ten feet." Chief Espinoza grinned. "That kid's got a great arm for a three-year-old."

"What about the little boy?" If tot number one— Carrie, he reminded himself—was raising all sorts of hell, it was probable the other was doing the same.

"Sound asleep. The little darling hasn't stirred since takeoff."

"Be grateful for small blessings," Matt murmured, turning back around to face the console. "Do your best, Load. I have the utmost confidence in you."

The sound that came over Matt's earphones wasn't exactly an acknowledgment of the compliment. Matt forgot about the load and his problems as he and the copilot spent a few minutes doing pilot stuff. A few minutes, no more, and then there was nothing to take his mind off the pretty little redhead with her screaming child.

He used his radio and called back to the load. Yes, the child was still screaming. Louder, if that was possible . . . and Load was convinced it was possible.

It was time to solve the problem. Matt turned to his copilot. "Rick, I don't suppose you had any money left over after you bought Emily that pearl necklace?"

The copilot raised a single brow and shuddered. "I barely had enough left to eat with the last four days.

I sure hope my wife appreciates that fact when I arrive home half-emaciated."

Matt chuckled. "More to the point, I suppose, is what are you taking the kids? Twinkies left over from your flight lunch?"

"They're not even that lucky," Rick said, his gaze flicking over the instrument panel before returning to Matt's. "This trip, all those little monsters are getting is the complimentary pad of paper and the pen I ripped off from the hotel in Hawaii."

"Cheap, Rick. Very cheap."

"Tell me that again when you get married and have kids. Just because you're footloose and fancy-free and don't have anyone to spend your money on doesn't mean the rest of us can't skimp once in a while."

"I bought my sister and her new husband a wedding present," Matt said in defense of his spending habits.

"It's not like she's expects you to bring her something every time you go on a trip," Rick pointed out. "Getting married is something your sister will do only once."

Twice, actually. But the first time didn't count, not really. This time, Maggie was truly in love. Matt had met Will and knew without a single doubt that his sister had found a man who would still be with her when they were both old and gray.

He smiled out at the encroaching darkness, trying to picture his blond, vivacious sister forty years hence. Maybe by that time, Will would have talked her into driving something besides that Volkswagen beetle she'd had for the past ten years.

Then again, maybe not. Matt swallowed a chuckle and returned to the subject at hand. "You mean you didn't buy them anything?"

"I'm going to be flying for a long time, Matt. It's appropriate that I set a precedent for what's to come." Rick grinned. "My family has to know that I'm out here working and not just flying all over the world on one endless shopping trip."

"So what's with the pearls?"

"Give me a break. It's our anniversary." Rick pulled a stick of gum from his pocket and folded it into his mouth. "What's it to you, anyway? You think I'm neglecting my kids?"

Before Matt could reply, the engineer cut in. "Don't be dense, sir," he said, without any pretense at respect. "He's looking for a pacifier."

"Pacifier?" Rick repeated, puzzled.

Matt shot the engineer a hopeful glance. "I don't suppose you have anything suitable, Carl?"

"Not a doll, boss," the engineer replied. "But I do happen to have a stuffed koala bear that I picked up in Australia last week. I was saving it for my niece's Christmas present."

"It's not even Valentine's Day yet, Carl. I'll give you double what you paid."

"Kind of thought you'd feel like that."

Money changed hands, and Matt told him to make finding that bear a priority.

Still, it took time. First, the engineer had to wait for the scanner to come forward and take over his seat. Then he retreated to the bowels of the aircraft in search of the crew's baggage. Since all the bags were standard issue and therefore identical, he had to check all the tags before he found the right one.

Thirty minutes later, Matt opened the door from the cockpit. A shrill scream penetrated the air around him, and he shuddered, just barely pushing aside the temptation to dig his own earplugs out of his pocket. He wouldn't be long, he reassured himself. He'd just give Carrie the bear and get back to the flight deck, where he could watch the stars and listen to the muffled roar of the engines.

After climbing down the ladder from the flight deck, Matt tucked the koala bear under his arm and strode down the aisle. The small family had moved to the rear of the aircraft while the rest of the passengers had banded together in the seats closest to the forward bulkhead—out of range but certainly not out of earshot. Looking over the backs of the seats, Matt saw tot number one as she struggled furiously in the redhead's arms. He wondered how long she'd be able to hold on—the mother, not the child.

As the airline-type seats faced backward, the redhead didn't see him until he circled around in front of her. It was obvious that while Carrie was prepared to scream all night, the mother was getting just a touch ragged. Her green eyes were red and swollen from fatigue, her hair a tangle of curls, her skin flushed from the effort she was exerting to keep the child from tumbling to the floor.

Matt wondered again where her husband was and why he'd sent her off alone with the children.

Carrie screamed and pounded chubby fists against her mother, who held her close with one arm and stroked her back with the other. The redhead looked up at Matt over the child's head.

"I'm sorry, Colonel," she said, shifting Carrie in her arms in an attempt to stop her from kicking the sleeping boy in the next seat. "But I did try to warn you."

There was no trace of her former belligerence in her expression, although Matt credited that lack to a depletion of resources. He hunkered down onto his heels and held out the bear. "I don't know if this will help . . ."

Surprise flickered in her eyes, followed by a softening that made the breath catch in his throat. Without wasting time, she took the koala and stuck it in Carrie's face. It took the child about three seconds to realize there was a furry addition to their huddle.

The howling stopped. Carrie rubbed her fisted hand across her eyes and snaked an arm around the bear, pulling it close. Sticking her thumb into her mouth, she shut her eyes and burrowed against her mother's chest.

Blessed silence filled the hull—although Matt thought he heard a smattering of applause from the other end of the aircraft. He didn't dare say anything, though, for fear of waking Carrie, and the redhead looked too tired to speak. She tried anyway.

"Thank you, Colonel," she said in a hushed voice. "I think we can rest assured that she'll sleep for hours now." Shifting the child in her arms, she tried to lift her into the next seat.

It was obvious that her strength was nearly gone, because the best she could do was get Carrie as far as the armrest. Matt intervened, as much out of fear that Carrie would awaken as anything else. He took the sleeping child in his big hands, cradling her across his arm as the redhead tucked blankets into the corners of the seat. Together, they propped Carrie against the blankets, then wedged several more around her small body. Matt dug into the cracks between the seats until he found the seat belt and snapped it shut. Quietly.

"How much longer before we get wherever we're going?"

He looked up to find the woman watching him. "About five hours, give or take. And we're going to Wake Island."

Her brows drew together in concern. "What's wrong with Guam?"

"The typhoon looks like it might go there next. Wake Island is our next-best choice."

"Oh." She looked appalled at the lack of options offered in this aircraft that was cruising thirty thousand feet above the Pacific.

"Your daughter has an impressive set of lungs," Matt said, unwilling for some reason to leave, even though his mission had been accomplished.

"If Carrie were my daughter, I'm not sure having an impressive set of lungs is something I'd take pride in."

"She's not yours?"

The woman laughed softly. "Uh-uh."

"Oh." His brows lifted curiously.

"Neither is Keith," she added, glancing over at the other sleeping child. "I've been their nanny for the last three months, Colonel." She yawned unselfconsciously and stretched her arms high above her head.

"Matt," he said.

Her eyebrows arched in surprise. "Matt?"

"He nodded. "Matt Cooper."

She smiled. "Well, Matt Cooper, it seems I owe you one."

One what? he wondered. "Does this mean you're not angry with me for . . . er, helping you aboard earlier?"

She appeared to be considering it. "I was never angry, Colonel—"

"Matt."

She bowed her head for a moment. When she lifted her gaze to his again, he saw a touch of laughter in her eyes. "I was never angry, Matt. It was just that I knew better than you what lay in store for all of us if we left without the doll. My fault, really. I should have checked before we left the terminal."

Matt's gaze slid over the sleeping children. "I think getting these two in and out of that bus presented enough of a challenge as it was."

She reached over and gently pushed a lock of hair from Carrie's face. "They're really not as bad as they acted earlier. It's just that they were so frightened."

"Where are their parents?" A much better question, he thought, than the one he'd been asking himself from the moment he saw her. *Where was her husband?* Yes, he liked this question much better.

"In Hong Kong. They flew out two days ago for a conference." She yawned again, covering her mouth with fingers that were long and slender. And ringless. He should have noticed that earlier. She smiled over the yawn. "Sorry about that, Col—Matt. It seems like I've hardly slept since they left."

A hint. Yes, Matt could take a hint. The redhead wanted to get some sleep. Glancing at the now-quiet children, he could hardly blame her for jumping at the opportunity. Standing, he snagged an extra blanket from the next row of seats and draped it across her shoulders. The small act of intimacy brought with it a rush of unfamiliar emotion. He tried to ignore it.

"Thanks," she said, tucking her legs beneath her. "For the koala too."

"Just let Chief Espinoza know if you need anything."

She smiled sleepily.

"I'll leave you to it, then."

She closed her eyes. Matt waited for a moment—just to make sure, he told himself. Sure of what, he really didn't know. But his reluctance to leave her was a very real feeling that he couldn't shake.

Her eyes remained closed. Sighing, Matt turned to make his way back up the aisle.

He wanted to know her name.

"Jenfer, I gotta go."

Matt's head whipped around. Tot number two—Keith, he thought he remembered her saying—was sitting up and poking the redhead in the arm.

"Jenfer," he wailed plaintively. "Wake up. I want bafwom!"

There was a nervous rustling at the front of the plane, and Matt knew the other passengers were fearing another lengthy outburst. He wondered if the engineer had any more toys tucked in his B4 bag.

The redhead responded slowly. Matt watched as her fingers first fumbled with her seat belt, then with Keith's. He couldn't bear to look into her eyes, though, because he'd seen her exhaustion and there wasn't anything he could do about it.

He had an airplane to fly. Turning away, he continued up the aisle.

Jenfer, the child had said. Jennifer? A name to go with the face.

The remainder of the flight was long and uneventful. Matt didn't leave the flight deck again, but continued to receive a steady stream of reports from the crew.

The two children alternated naps, one resting as

the other prowled the aircraft. There was no more screaming, although Matt felt sure Jennifer would be ready to do a little shouting herself by the time they came within spitting distance of Wake Island. Keeping a two- or three-year-old child buckled into his or her seat was a challenge of the highest order, an uphill battle that she fought for nearly five hours.

After Keith succeeded in locking himself in the bathroom, the loadmaster assigned one of the airmen to guard the door. It would have been more productive for the airman to help Jennifer keep the kids corralled, but baby-sitting was above and beyond the call of duty. So Jennifer was left to struggle with the kids and the airman made sure the bathroom stayed available for the use of all passengers.

The hours dragged. Matt traded jokes with the crew and used every excuse in the book to check up on the trio in back without being too obvious about his interest. He was pretty sure the crew knew, anyway, but were tactful enough not to harass him. The reports came more frequently, though, and with less attention to the children's antics and more to the steadily deteriorating condition of their nanny.

Matt worried, but knew that there wasn't a thing he could do about it. He thought about offering to give the children a tour of the flight deck, but he'd have to make the same offer to the rest of the passengers, and frankly, it had been a long day and the crew wasn't up for a steady stream of visitors.

It was a long flight.

Three

He lost track of her when they landed at Wake Island. By the time he finished his duties on the flight deck and checked in with base operations, she had disappeared.

Jennifer of the spine-tickling voice had gone her own way. He could find out which quarters she'd been allocated, but what was the use? He was leaving the next day. And the chances that he'd touch down again at Pilau were next to nil. In another three months or so, he'd be retiring from the air force and his days of flying around the world and the Pacific in particular would be over.

Perhaps it was just as well. Jennifer was the kind of woman he'd always avoided—and not because she had the words *Marry Me* etched in neon on her forehead. After years of practice, he could spot one of those coming a block away.

No, Jennifer wasn't in that category at all . . . which made it even worse. Matt had a gut feeling that that was how he would feel if he spent too much time with her. Already he was tempted to find a mirror and double-check his own forehead.

He hardly knew her at all. She lived on Pilau. It would be best if he avoided seeing her again.

End of discussion.

He ate a quick dinner, then returned to his quarters. Falling asleep was simple once he made up his mind to awaken for an early breakfast.

Perhaps the kids were early risers too.

He wondered if the inability to stick to a decision was an early sign of senility.

The next morning, Matt breakfasted on a couple cans of juice from the machine down the hall, but otherwise hid out in his room.

"You're not hiding," he told himself as he stood at his window. "You're just enjoying the peace and quiet while you've got the chance."

Talking to himself was a by-product of having lived so much of his life alone. He'd been doing it so long, he hardly realized it. He stretched and took a last sip of the coffee he'd made.

"Face it, Matt," he said impatiently. "If she lived somewhere normal, like Albuquerque or Milwaukee, you'd be out there looking for her."

Somewhere normal. Like Tacoma, Washington, where he lived.

Matt wondered where Jennifer had lived before she went to Pilau. He couldn't place her accent. Hadn't given it much thought, really, because that sexy rasp had distracted him from the first moment he'd heard it.

She was an American, though. And her last name was Delaney. He knew that much because Chief Espinoza had had to check everyone's passports.

Jennifer Delaney from Pilau. Kind of hard to trace if she moved away.

Not too easy if she stayed, but not impossible. How many Jennifers could there be on an island as small as that?

He shook his head. "Get a grip, cowboy. You have no business chasing after a girl who's only half your age . . . if that." Her skin was so fresh and beautiful, he remembered. Even with rings of exhaustion below her eyes, she'd been a pleasure to look at. But skin like that only blessed the very young. Matt wondered if she was at least twenty-one.

Too bad he hadn't thought to ask Chief Espinoza how old she was, because it seemed she got younger every time he thought about her.

He didn't have the nerve to ask now.

Matt went into the bathroom and rinsed out his portable coffee machine. Looking into the mirror at his gray eyes and the odd strand of gray in his blond hair, he wondered if he looked his age. Forty-three. He didn't feel forty-three.

Still, he wished forty-three was closer to the twenties. Shaking his head, he dried off the coffee machine and repacked it in its case. The telephone rang as he was tucking it back into his bag.

It was Rick. "How about a little tennis? Loser buys lunch."

Matt checked his watch. They had six hours before show time. "You looking for revenge after that beating you took on Guam?"

"I'm young enough to believe that crushing defeats at the hand of the aircraft commander should be allocated to goodwill. The question is, can you do it twice?"

"If you're sure your ego can stand the answer to that, I'll meet you in ten minutes."

Putting down the phone, Matt said a silent thanks to his copilot. Staying away from Jennifer would be easier if he kept busy.

Forgetting her wasn't going to be as simple. A little like yanking out gray hairs, he imagined. He could make the gray and the thoughts go away . . . but only temporarily, until they came back, until something happened to remind him of her.

"That's right, Matt," he told himself. "Keep your gray hair and Jennifer in the same thought frame and you won't have any trouble."

He changed into tennis gear and went outside to deal with a copilot who didn't realize age was no deterrent to skill.

Six–two, six–three. They were both sweating when

they walked away from the clay court, but it was Rick who bought lunch at the snack bar.

Matt went back to his quarters and stayed there until it was time to catch the crew bus back to the flight line. Under his hands, the Starlifter lumbered down the runway before lifting gracefully into the sky. The late-afternoon sunshine glinted off the massive wings as he turned the aircraft in the direction of Hawaii.

Hawaii, then home.

He thought of Jennifer and wondered how long she'd be stuck on Wake Island before it was safe to return to Pilau.

Already overloaded with aircrews passing through, Hickam Air Force Base sent Matt's crew to a Waikiki hotel instead of quartering them on base. No one complained, of course. With two days to kill before they had a plane and a mission bound for Tacoma, it was much nicer being in downtown Hawaii where they could put on flowered shirts and act like tourists, even if dawn was history by the time they checked into the hotel.

After a short "night's" sleep, Matt forced himself out of bed. It was already early afternoon, and if he didn't start now, his body clock would never get back in gear. Alone, he wandered through the hotel's ground-floor mall, wearing the new shirt he'd bought at the front end of the mission. It was blue with purple highlights—just loud enough to make him feel like he belonged among the throng of holidaymakers. He wore cheap sandals purchased several trips ago in the Philippines and his legs were bare and tan beneath khaki shorts.

It was a beautiful afternoon. Slipping on his sunglasses, he stepped outside and decided to walk down to the beach. Maybe buy a fresh pineapple to take home. Some Hawaiian bread.

His stomach grumbled, and he realized he'd be better off eating a little something before he bought more food than he could possibly carry home with him. If his memory served, there was a little kiosk around the corner that served fresh—

The unexpected sting of gooey ice smushing into his kneecap nearly crippled him.

Startled out of his menu-centered thoughts, Matt came to an abrupt halt and stared downward. A disgusting combination of black-flecked green stuff smeared atop a blob of orange was beginning to slide down his shin. Without budging, he adjusted his gaze to the young child who stood just inches away, an empty ice-cream cone in his hand and tears gathering in his eyes. As he stared the child leaned toward Matt and attempted to retrieve the best part of his treat.

"No, don't do that, darling. We'll get you another." A slender hand reached down to stop the child. To stop Keith.

Shivers that had nothing to do with the slimy mess on his leg zipped along Matt's spine. Slowly, he lifted his gaze several feet, taking his time because today she was wearing a tight wraparound dress that hugged her hips and sculpted her breasts. She, too, wore an island print, yellow and orange flowers that should have clashed with her hair but didn't. The deep red auburn tones were as rich and lustrous as he remembered, the thick curls only slightly less unruly but no less beautiful than the picture in his mind.

She still looked as tired as she had on the Star-lifter. He was wondering if she'd gotten any rest at all when she glanced up and recognition flared in her gaze. He could have sworn she was happy to see him, but whatever it was that made him think that disappeared quickly beneath a cloak of reserve.

"Hello, Jennifer."

"Hello to you, Colonel Coop—"

"Matt," he interrupted. It was important that she call him that.

"Matt," she said softly. "Fancy running into you in Waikiki!"

He grinned. The sound of her husky voice wrapping around his name pleased him. He almost forgot the slime on his leg as he stood with her in the sunshine, in a place he'd never liked as much as he did at that moment.

She smiled, too, brilliantly—apologetically—and delved into her handbag with one hand as she held her own cone in the other. "I'd let Keith clean it up, but I don't think you'd survive the experience."

Matt grinned. "It's nothing a stroll in the surf won't fix." He took careful, mincing steps over to the curb, where he allowed the blob of ice cream to fall into the gutter. Using the tissue she handed him, he mopped up the worst of the mess. The tissue went into a nearby bin before he returned to where Jennifer and Keith were waiting. The little boy was sobbing quietly as he stared at Matt's knees, making Matt wonder if he should apologize for walking into his ice cream.

Hunkering down on his heels, he caught Keith's gaze with his own and smiled. "Remember me, Keith? From the airplane?"

Another sob, and Keith buried his face against Jennifer's thigh.

"Don't be frightened, love," she soothed. "This man is the pilot from the airplane. He's not angry about the ice cream."

Obviously, Keith didn't care if Matt was angry or not, because he cried louder and screamed "ith kwem!"

Matt got the picture. "Let's go get another," he suggested.

Keith looked at him, bottom lip trembling, and nodded vigorously.

Rising to his feet, Matt suddenly remembered tot number one. "Where's Carrie?" Had Jennifer lost one of the Fearsome Twosome in the crowds? He didn't think so, because she'd be frantic instead of smiling.

Jennifer pointed to a table just a few feet away. There, under the awning of the ice-cream shop, Carrie was zealously spooning up great blobs of pink ice cream from the bowl in front of her. The koala watched from a perch on the same table, a safe distance from the action.

"Keith wanted a cone, of course," Jennifer said. "And he wouldn't sit down because cones are made for walking." She chuckled and bent down to the boy. "Would you like to go inside with Colonel Cooper and get another ice cream, darling?"

Keith sniffled and stuck his hand up to meet Matt's. "Kernel get ith kwem." His hand now as sticky as his leg, Matt shuffled alongside the small boy into the shop.

Leadership by example. It was one of the first tenets of command, and Matt couldn't believe it wouldn't work now. Picking Keith up and settling him in the crook of his elbow, he ordered himself a bowl of ice cream and asked Keith if he'd like a bowl or a cone. When the child asked for a bowl, Matt patted himself on the back for applying everything he'd learned over the past twenty years in a potentially critical situation.

He wouldn't for a second acknowledge the possibility that Keith was simply learning from experience.

They rejoined the women—girls really, when one considered the younger couldn't be more than three and the other looked like a teenager, what with her tongue licking the ice cream with girlish delight and laughing as she shared a joke with Carrie.

Matt felt older by the minute. "You look about sixteen right now."

Jennifer looked up at him in amused surprise. "You don't sound as though that makes you very happy."

He lifted Keith onto a chair, then took the seat next to Jennifer. "I feel like a lech," he growled, sticking his spoon into the ice cream and reaching over to steady Keith's bowl as the child dug into his own. "A *very old* lech."

"A lech?"

He nodded. "I have thoughts about you that are

less than admirable, given the differences in our ages."

Jennifer stared at him across the top of her ice cream, her gaze softening in what could only be described as pleasure. "Would it make you feel better if I told you I was old enough to vote?"

He shook his head. "Not much. That still puts a twenty-odd-year gap between us."

She stopped eating and leaned forward, just an inch or so . . . enough to enable her to lower her voice so that the children wouldn't hear. "Colonel Cooper, why does it matter how old I am?"

"Matt," he said.

"Matt." A whisper of sound . . . enchanting him.

He shoved his ice cream aside, but didn't loosen his grasp of the boy's. Dropping his own voice a level or so, he said, "I knew when I left Wake Island that I'd never see you again. But now that I have, it would make me feel a hell of a lot better to know that I won't be spending the rest of my life fantasizing about a woman who is young enough to be my daughter."

A slow, easy smile lifted the corners of her mouth. "Would the fact that my thirtieth birthday is next week make your fantasy bearable?"

It would.

His gaze narrowed on her lips. Such a pretty mouth, he thought, full of lush promises of nights of pleasure. He groaned audibly and remembered where they were. And who they were with. He checked the boy next to him and was pleased to discover he was happily slopping down the ice cream. All over him, of course, but Matt expected that was the way all kids ate. He hoped Jennifer had the sense to send their clothes out instead of trying to do the wash herself. She was exhausted from two long plane trips.

He wanted to hold her and let her sleep.

Nonsense, he told himself. *Just because you're with her now doesn't mean you'll see her again once the ice cream is gone.*

"I don't suppose you can prove your age?" he

asked quietly. Why did she have to live clear the hell out in the middle of the Pacific?

"You're no better than a bartender," she griped with her smile intact. Digging into her purse, she pulled out a passport and opened it in front of his eyes. Jennifer Adams Delaney. And, yes, it actually supported her claim to be twenty-nine.

He lifted his gaze to hers and asked her what she was doing for dinner. Even though she looked as though she needed a nap more than food, he couldn't bring himself to offer that.

She didn't know him well enough to realize he would be making a genuine offer.

She laughed and glanced at the children, who were beginning to fidget. "What do you expect I'm doing? Feeding these two, of course."

He wasn't a quitter. "If I can find a baby-sitter, will you have dinner with me?"

Her brows arched. "A baby-sitter I can trust?"

He nodded. "Guaranteed. A person that I know."

"Know how well?"

"Better than I know you."

She laughed again. "You could pull a bum off the street that you know better than me!"

He pretended offense. "I don't know any bums. Not in Hawaii, anyway."

"So if it's not a bum . . . ?"

"Trust me, Jennifer. I'll find a baby-sitter who will meet with your strict requirements."

Her eyes took on a speculative expression as she appeared to give his invitation serious thought. "All right, Colonel. It's a deal. I'll be ready at seven." She gave him her hotel and room number.

They were staying in the same hotel.

"I'll book a table for the dining room on the top floor," he said as he stood up. "That way, the sitter will be able to find you if he has any trouble."

"He?"

Matt ignored her surprised exclamation and stooped down to say one more thing. "And Jennifer?"

"Yes?"

"Call me Matt."

Matt rapped his knuckles on the door of his copilot's room, totally ignoring the Do Not Disturb sign hanging from the knob. No answer. He knocked again, louder.

A muffled voice responded. "Go 'way. Can't you read?"

"It's Matt Cooper. I need to talk with you, Captain." Using rank instead of a name would get a better response, he figured. He was willing to use any trick in the book to get some time alone with Jennifer. Ten seconds passed before he heard Rick fumbling with the dead bolt.

Bleary eyes stared out at him through a six-inch crack. "What's up?"

Matt grinned and gently pushed the door open. Inside the room, he pulled open the drapes to let in the late-afternoon sunshine. "You shouldn't sleep like this, Rick. You know you'll never get your time zones straight if you don't make an effort to stay awake during the day."

Dressed in shorts, Rick crawled onto the bed and fell back against the pillows. "You woke me up to give me a lesson in travel techniques?"

Matt threw a pile of clothes from one chair onto another and sat down. "Sorry about this, Rick, but I need a favor."

Rick pushed himself up onto his elbows. "What kind of favor?"

Matt weighed his words carefully. "First, let me tell you what I'm going to do for you."

"Let me sleep?"

"Not now. But how would you like to have the left seat to yourself for the trip home?" The person who sat in the left was essentially in charge. The one in the right would do most of the grunt work, leaving the fun stuff for the left. The real flying. On this trip, they'd mostly traded off—except for the flight into

Pilau, when Matt's experience had dictated he be in charge.

The trip as a whole was under Matt's command, so it was his decision who got to do which takeoffs and which landings. He'd taken the last leg from Wake Island to Hawaii for himself, needing the activity to focus his thoughts away from Jennifer. The trip from Hawaii would require two takeoffs and landings: Hawaii to Travis Air Force Base in northern California, then Travis to McChord in Washington.

He was offering all the "stick time" to Rick.

Rick's eyes narrowed suspiciously. "What do I have to do?"

Matt sweetened the pot. "I'll also buy you dinner tomorrow night, anywhere you like."

Rick sat up. "This is beginning to sound serious."

"And I'll spring for presents for your kids. I remember you pointing out those inflatable dolphins on our trip out. Wouldn't you like to take a couple home with you?"

"Sorry, Colonel." Rick shook his head regretfully. "I think you've overestimated my abilities. Why don't you check with Superman? He's in a room just a few doors down. I'm sure he'll be more up for whatever task you've got in mind."

Matt grinned. "I haven't even told you what I want."

"For everything you're giving away, I know better than to even consider it."

"Even if I told you it would only take about three hours of your time?"

Rick rubbed sleep from his eyes. "Three hours when?"

"Tonight. Seven o'clock." Matt waited for the bribe to sink in. The left seat. Dinner. Dolphins. He'd add to it if he had to.

Rick swung his legs over the side of the bed and rested his forearms on his thighs. "Put me out of my misery, Matt. Just tell me who I have to kill and get it over with."

Matt took the plunge. "I need you to baby-sit so that I can take Jennifer out to dinner. That's all."

Rick's eyebrows rose expressively. "Baby-sit? Who's Jennifer?"

Before Matt could answer, understanding flashed in Rick's eyes. "The redhead." He stood up and stretched. "Of course. I should have realized this was serious business."

"Will you do it?" Matt held his breath.

Rick went to the window and squinted into the slanted rays of the afternoon sun. "Who's going to flight-plan for the trip home?"

Matt sighed. "I am."

"And weather? You think you can handle that too?"

Flight plan and weather. Both of them big jobs that were faster and easier for two. "I can handle that too."

"And—"

"Don't push your luck, Rick." Matt put a lid on the demands before they got out of hand. "You've got my best offer. Do we have a deal?" He rose from the chair and waited.

Rick turned from the window and held out his hand. "Deal."

Matt breathed easily for the first time in ten minutes.

Four

Her smile was warm and friendly, and melted his insides like a hot iron on wax.

It was a promising beginning, Matt thought as he introduced Rick and Jennifer.

He waited by the door as she reeled off a list of do's and don'ts to Uncle Ricky, taking pleasure in her husky voice and looking forward to the moment when he'd have her all to himself.

After what seemed like an aeon, she ran out of instructions and just stood there, watching, as Uncle Ricky began stuffing the kids into their bathing suits. Swimming, the young captain said, was precisely what these two balls of energy needed. Swimming, then dinner. After that, he pronounced, they'd sleep the night away.

Matt just prayed the kids would stop shy of drowning his copilot, because sudden death at the hands of toddlers would be hell to explain to their squadron commander.

But Uncle Ricky seemed to know what he was doing. When Jennifer still appeared reluctant to leave, Matt put his hand on her shoulder, nudging her toward the door—and the satin of her bare shoulder burned him. The fire was an erotic flame unlike anything he'd ever experienced.

She didn't know, of course, what made him jerk

his hand from her shoulder and avoid touching her as they made their way to the restaurant. She shot him a strange look, though, her eyes filled with a combination of curiosity and amusement.

He felt like a schoolboy on his first date.

His gaze fell on the blue silk gown that bared her shoulders and arms to the soft caress of the night's breeze as they traversed the rooftop patio. If she were any other woman, he wouldn't have hesitated to lay his arm across her shoulders and draw her close to his side, as if to protect her from the nonexistent cold.

Instead, he walked slightly behind her, resisting temptation. When he held her body against his, it would be an act of deliberate intent.

Matt swallowed hard, his fingers tugging at the knot of his tie because it was suddenly too tight, too confining. He stopped short of taking the thing off, and settled for flexing his shoulders beneath his cashmere sport jacket.

They reached the restaurant and he held the door for her. She slipped past him, and her subtle fragrance of flowers and spring imprinted itself upon his senses. Permanently, he imagined. They waited for a moment in the foyer, cloaked in a silence that was seductively comfortable. He resumed watching her, a pastime that was fast becoming an obsession.

Her sun-warmed skin glowed in the light of dozens of candles, her hair a burnished flame of another kind. His gaze dropped a few inches, gliding past the even pulse at her throat. Only a hint of her breasts was revealed above the tight bodice of her gown. A hint of perfection. Her breasts weren't overly generous in size, but the modesty with which she didn't display them was enticingly sexy.

The maître d' arrived to usher them to the window-side table Matt had reserved earlier. Beyond the windows, he knew the lights of Honolulu glittered like a fairyland. He'd brought her there because he'd thought the view would please her.

For himself, watching Jennifer was as much visual

entertainment as he could handle. He didn't spare the view a single glance, but instead watched her as she followed the maître d' across the room.

The full skirt of her dress swirled over her hips and came to a stop at least six inches above her knees. Her legs were slender and shapely, an opinion clearly shared by every other man in the restaurant, because they, too, were following her progress with rapt attention. When the maître d' stopped at their table, Matt elbowed him aside and held her chair for her. As she settled into it he was relieved that at least half of her was now hidden from sight. The other men would stop gawking any minute.

They didn't, though, not right away. From the waist up, Jennifer was still a magnet for the eyes. With her hair caught up into a loose knot at the back of her head and her skin a healthy glow that didn't owe its beauty to cosmetics or jewels, she caught the attention of nearly everyone in the room and then proceeded to ignore it, as if she didn't know anyone was staring.

As he pushed in her chair she lifted her face and gave him a shy smile, and he realized she was truly unaware of the stir she'd caused. It startled him and pleased him in the same instant. Taking his own seat, he scowled at the room in general, surprising himself with his reaction. He'd never minded before when the woman he escorted received a surfeit of attention. It was one of the hazards of dating a beautiful woman.

Tonight, though, he minded.

Looking across the table at Jennifer, he wondered how he'd ever imagined she was anything less than a raving beauty. Pretty, not gorgeous, he remembered thinking.

He'd been wrong.

"You're staring at me."

He made a stab at recovering his famous calm. "Perhaps if you didn't look quite so beautiful, I wouldn't be staring." Even though the lights were low, he detected a faint blush creeping into her cheeks. It pleased him to know he could affect her too. He watched with satisfaction as she nibbled on her lower lip, a sign of nerves she couldn't quite control.

"It's the dress," she said, looking down at it as her fingers smoothed across the silk that rested between her breasts. "I just bought it this afternoon and the saleswoman told me it was a knockout."

"I wasn't talking about the dress."

"You don't like it?" Her brows shot up in surprise. "But I thought—"

"Forget the dress, Jennifer. It's how you look in it that's got my attention."

"Oh?" Her lashes fluttered, and he couldn't decide if she was flirting or genuinely embarrassed by his words. A little of both, he decided, smiling.

"You didn't look at me like that when we were on Pilau," she said.

"I didn't know I could." There was a husky catch in his voice, which he stopped to clear before going on. "On Pilau, you had two kids hanging on your hips."

She laughed, slender fingers reaching up to toy with a strand of hair at her nape. "I have to admit that I certainly wasn't at my best that day. Between Typhoon Harry and the children, I probably looked ready for a long winter's rest."

He shook his head. "That's not what I meant. I thought the kids were yours."

"I know."

He saw a look of feminine pleasure cross her face, and knew that she was enjoying his attention as he was enjoying her presence. He would have said more, but the waiter arrived and involved them both in an endless recitation of what was available, fresh, or just plain special. Matt watched Jennifer as she paid rapt attention to every detail. With her chin resting on her hands and her gaze steady on the waiter, she looked as though this was the best entertainment she'd had in a year.

Watching her, Matt had to agree.

She asked for soda water instead of a cocktail or

glass of wine. Matt doubled the order and sent the waiter away looking distinctly unhappy. Matt guessed the man had figured them for champagne.

"I don't mind if you prefer something stronger," Jennifer said, putting her menu aside without looking at it.

He shrugged. "I try not to drink much when I'm traveling. It makes it easier to adjust to all the changes in time zones. I will have a little wine with dinner, though. Join me?"

She shook her head. "I'll pass, thank you."

He arched his brows curiously. "You think I'll get you drunk and seduce you?"

"Seduce me?" A giggle burbled past her lips, and he was charmed, her sweet husky voice an erotic stroke of magic that couldn't be dispelled by her disbelief. Hell, yes, he wanted to seduce her.

It was only fair. She'd already seduced him, with her voice, her body . . . her innocence.

He knew she was innocent even though he couldn't understand why or how. Not necessarily virginal, but innocent all the same.

He adored her for it.

"You don't want me to seduce you?" he asked, leaning back in his chair to take the threat from his words. Her breath caught in her throat and he watched, fascinated, as the delicate pulse beat furiously at the base of her throat. She was intrigued by his teasing, he could tell, her expression a confusion of excitement and doubt.

She let the doubt sway her. "When I was eighteen, I drank three glasses of champagne at my aunt's wedding."

"And?"

Her gaze flickered across the room before returning to him. "And I disgraced myself thoroughly," she said, grimacing. "I haven't had a drink since."

He laughed. "You carry a grudge a long time."

The waiter appeared with their soda water and stayed to take their orders. Jennifer systematically went through the menu and ordered a bizarre combination of foods that she explained were all things she'd never tried before. While Matt's own order was more conventional, the waiter drifted away looking as though he'd forgiven them for not ordering champagne.

Matt turned back to Jennifer and watched as she squeezed her wedge of lemon into her soda water. A little thing, squeezing a lemon, he thought, and was startled to realize how much attention he was paying to these little things.

He flicked his own lemon straight into his soda and took a sip. "I've been wondering all afternoon what you're doing in Hawaii."

"I'm taking Carrie and Keith to Seattle. The air force was kind enough to give us a ride off Wake Island yesterday morning. I booked us tickets on a commercial flight early tomorrow."

Seattle. Also known as the Emerald City—and it was just a few miles north of his home. An hour's drive, give or take.

The possibilities were intriguing.

"Why Seattle?" he asked casually.

"The children have an aunt there." She rested her chin on one hand and stared at him across the dancing flame of the candle. "By the time I got hold of their parents in Hong Kong, it was old news that Typhoon Harry made quite a mess of things on Pilau. They decided that as long as we were already on Wake Island, it would make more sense to take the kids to Seattle until things were settled enough for them to go back home."

"How long will you stay, do you think?"

"At least a couple of weeks," she said eagerly. "Long enough for me to get a chance to see the sights, I hope."

"You've never been to Washington State?"

"Until three months ago, I'd only been out of Montana twice in my entire life. Once to ski at Jackson Hole, Wyoming. The other to go to a friend's wedding in Minnesota."

"That's it?" He'd heard of people who never

strayed far from home. Jennifer just didn't look like someone who'd be satisfied with that kind of life—no matter how big and beautiful Montana was.

"My father worked for the State Parks and Recreation Department," she explained, "and couldn't understand why anyone would want or need to leave Montana for vacation. Since I went to a local college, there weren't that many opportunities to cross the border."

"Pilau is a long way from Montana."

"In more ways than one," she agreed, her eyes reflecting her enthusiasm. "Back home, we ate beef and lamb. The only fish we got was a choice of trout or trout. Anything more exotic was what they like to call fresh frozen—anywhere from three days to three months old. On Pilau, it's twenty kinds of fish that are only hours old, if that."

"Yeah, but I bet you can't get a good steak on Pilau."

"I've had good steak for thirty years. It'll be a while before I miss it." She folded her arms on the table and leaned forward, as though she were going to share a colossal secret. "Did you realize that even in the middle of summer, most of the fruits and vegetables we get in Montana have to be trucked in all the way from California?"

He smothered a grin and shook his head. No, he hadn't realized it.

"For the last three months," she went on, "I've eaten fruit that I'd never even heard of before. And most of it I picked myself!"

You would have thought she'd discovered gold. Perhaps, he mused, she had. Through her eyes, he could almost see the eighteen-carat sparkle for himself.

She barely paused for a breath before continuing. "And there are so many other things that are different and exciting about living on an island. Montana is wool and Gore-Tex. Pilau is cotton and bare skin. Snow skiing versus waterskiing. Long winter nights in front of a roaring fire as opposed to midnight walks on the beach. In Montana, you can drive for hours without seeing a single sign of civilization. On Pilau, you can drive around the entire island a dozen times between lunch and dinner."

"Notice that you're back on the subject of food?"

She laughed. "I like to eat. I guess it shows."

His gaze drifted over the soft swell of her breasts. "Not so's you'd notice."

The blush that he'd noticed earlier returned in full bloom. "I meant that I talk a lot about food," she said softly.

"I know what you meant," he murmured, letting his gaze settle on her lips. Her mouth was such a temptation, one that he had no intention of resisting.

Later.

"All in all, it doesn't sound like you think much of Montana," he said.

She looked surprised. "On the contrary. I love it there. The mountains, the wide-open spaces. It's a beautiful place to live."

"So why'd you leave?"

"Montana, as wonderful as it is, is only a small piece of this world. There are a few thousand other pieces out there just waiting for me."

"You sound like you intend to see them all."

"Not all, perhaps," she admitted, "but not for lack of trying." She turned to look once again at the dramatic view of Waikiki at night and sighed. "I just wish we weren't leaving Hawaii tomorrow. When I flew through here on my way to Pilau, I didn't get out of the airport. This time, I've only made it a block or so away from the hotel."

"You can't change your plans?"

She shook her head, dragging her gaze from the window. "The kids need to get settled. All this traveling is beginning to make them cranky."

Matt personally thought their behavior that afternoon was light-years better than how they'd behaved on Pilau, but he didn't say it. Besides, he didn't want to talk about Carrie and Keith.

He wanted to know more about Jennifer. "What part of Montana are you from?"

"Billings."

He'd heard of it. Barely. A medium-sized town near the Wyoming border, if he was thinking of the right place. The woman he was beginning to know was thirty years old and filled with a thirst for travel that she was only now beginning to indulge. He wondered what or who had kept her from taking that first giant step that had landed her on Pilau.

The waiter arrived with their appetizers. Matt didn't take his gaze off Jennifer, trusting his peripheral vision to keep him from making a mess as he began to eat. His thoughts were occupied with trying to figure out how he could convince the squadron schedulers to let him stick around Tacoma for a couple of weeks. The trip next week to South America was a plum that every pilot in the squadron wanted. He didn't figure he'd have too much trouble finding someone to take his place.

He would take some time off, show Jennifer the beauty of the Puget Sound area, perhaps take her down to Oregon and let her see the dramatic coastline, which rivaled anything he'd seen in all his travels.

He tucked away the surprise for later and asked her why she hadn't left Montana earlier.

"I'd always planned to," she said as she spread lobster pâté on a piece of toasted bread. "Right after college, I was going to move to the West Coast." She sighed and smiled wistfully. "I wanted to live on the beach, learn to sail. Water-ski. Scuba dive. Hang gliding looked pretty good, although I have to admit I'm a little less taken with the idea now than I was eight years ago."

"What happened?"

"I think it's a case of having a better understanding of my own mortality," she said with an impish grin. "At twenty-two, hang gliding looked exciting. At thirty, it looks exciting and dangerous."

He bit off a laugh. "I meant what happened to keep you in Montana."

The grin faded. "My mom got sick. It was right after Dad died. I'd only been back from college for a month or so, was just beginning to get my plans in order. But she needed someone to take care of her." She held his gaze with a strength of will that dared him to pity her. "We couldn't afford a live-in nurse, and I don't have any brothers or sisters."

Eight years. A long time to suspend a dream. "You stayed because there wasn't anyone else to take care of her?"

"I stayed because I loved her." She pushed her empty plate aside and folded her hands on the white linen tablecloth. "I never stopped dreaming, though. When she died last year, I knew that I had to squeeze a lot of traveling into just a few years."

"Why the time limit?"

"Biological clock and all that. A family is important to me too. I figure I've got five or six years max before I have to get serious about it."

"I thought the 'life ends with marriage' syndrome was strictly a male attitude."

She grinned. "It is. I was referring to family life and how different it will be from the freedom I have as a single woman. Right now, depending on money and opportunity, I can go wherever and do whatever I wish."

Her viewpoint was remarkable only in that it mirrored his own—almost. Jennifer was looking forward to several years of the same freedom he had enjoyed for the last twenty, give or take a few restrictions by the United States Air Force. Now, though, he was preparing to settle down.

Too bad, he thought. Jennifer might be just the kind of woman with whom he could grow old and enjoy the process. Timing, he thought ruefully, was everything.

"So how did you end up on Pilau?" he asked. "It's not exactly the hub of the Pacific."

"Luck." She paused as the waiter arrived with the

main course. After he'd arranged everything to his satisfaction and melted into the background, she reminded Matt that he'd forgotten to order his wine.

"I think I'll give it a miss." He was unwilling to call the waiter back, because every interruption was time lost.

He watched Jennifer eat for a moment, enjoying her obvious pleasure with the shark steak and pasta. When he picked up his own fork and began his dinner, he realized the chef was truly inspired. It surprised him, because he'd eaten in this same restaurant on their last trip through and the food had been unremarkable at best.

Perhaps Jennifer's enthusiasm was contagious.

He was halfway through his meal before he stopped to ask her again how she'd managed to get a job on Pilau.

"It was simple, really," she said. "I just hooked up with an international placement agency and took the most interesting offer that came my way."

"But why a job as a nanny? You mentioned you went to college. Wasn't there something else you could have done?"

"A liberal arts education isn't all that marketable these days," she said with dry humor. "Besides, taking care of children is something I've always enjoyed. Back home, I sometimes watched the neighbors' kids when their regular baby-sitters weren't available. In return, there would always be someone to stay with Mom if I needed to be out at night."

He didn't want to know about those nights.

She told him anyway—sort of. "Charlie usually taught the night classes, though, and let me have the afternoon ones. Mom had a friend who liked to come and watch the soaps with her, which gave me several free hours most afternoons."

Matt kept a tight smile on his face. "What classes?" *And who the hell was Charlie?*

Jennifer looked up at him and blinked rapidly as though walking out of a dark theater into the bright light of day. Then she gave an embarrassed laugh, touching her napkin to her lips. "Sorry about that. Of course you don't know about the classes. It's just that I forget you don't know everything about me." She cocked her head. "Would it sound too corny if I told you I feel like I've known you a very long time?"

"Corny? No." He smiled at her. "I'd wish it were true . . . but for one thing."

"What's that?"

"If I'd known you a very long time, I wouldn't be sitting here wondering what our first kiss was going to be like."

Her gaze dropped from his, her thick, dark lashes hiding whatever she thought about that. Suddenly, she looked up again, stealing his breath with a look so frankly sensual it left him stunned.

"Matt?"

He swallowed hard, but could marshal no other response, not when she was heating his blood to previously unregistered levels. Her smile was wildly erotic as well, driving the rhythm of his heart into triple time.

She wet her lips and asked, "Do you always say outrageous things like that?"

"Sweet, you could give lessons in outrageous."

The blush was back, clearing all signs of sensual foreplay and leaving a clear, guileless expression in her emerald eyes.

Vamp or innocent? he wondered. Finding out should be an interesting voyage.

With a hard swallow for fortitude, he waded out of the erotic depths into safer shallows, knowing he'd dive back in before the night was done. "Now that we've got that settled . . ." he began, but was interrupted by her soft laugh. He shook his head and felt his own cheeks warm. He cleared his throat and tried again to take charge.

"Tell me about those classes."

She grinned. "Auto mechanics in winter, wildflowers of the west in spring, and underwater photography in the summer."

"Underwater photography in Montana?"

"You'd be surprised at the demand for that class. It's not so odd, if you think about it. Lots of people vacation in places where they can use the skill. Just because there's not much to photograph in an indoor pool in Montana doesn't mean the same principles don't apply."

The image of a dozen or more people taking pictures of each other at the bottom of a pool made him laugh. "Your leaving Montana must have left quite a void. Does this Charlie manage on his own now?"

She nodded, a hint of knowing humor lighting her gaze. "Charlie is my teacher and my friend. My father's friend, actually, but the bond passed to me when Dad died. He made sure I learned everything well enough so that I could help him teach. He thought I needed a hobby that would get me out of the house."

A teacher. Matt could handle that, he decided, almost embarrassed now at his flash of jealousy. He hoped she hadn't noticed. "You don't look like a mechanic," he said, thinking a trace of chauvinism would deflect the conversation away from Charlie.

She looked more amused than offended. "I decided when I was fifteen that one day, I'd drive from Alaska to the tip of Chile. It made sense to get prepared."

"You've never made the trip, though, have you?"

She shook her head. "I also haven't crossed it off my list."

"Exactly where is it on the list?"

Her brow furrowed as she concentrated. "Between exploring the beaches of the Seychelles and salmon fishing in Alaska, I think. At least that's where it was the last time I checked."

Her ambition filled him with awe. "The Seychelles should be fairly easy from Pilau. Speaking of which, how long do you plan to stay on Pilau?"

She twisted a bit of pasta around her fork and tucked it between her lips. "About a year, I think. I've checked with a travel agency, and I can get around the Pacific pretty well from there. If I keep the trips short enough and save my money in between, I should be able to do quite a lot." She shrugged and gave him a philosophical look. "I've only been there three months so far, though. Not long enough to get any vacation time."

"Do you have to work?"

She nodded. "Mom's illness ate up everything she had. Since I had to be more or less on call for her, I couldn't get a job."

He admired her for the matter-of-fact way she answered his question. It happened, that's the hand life had dealt her, there was no going back. Period.

She looked to the future with an enthusiasm he found invigorating. Infectious, almost. His response surprised him, because it had never occurred to him that he might have lost his own intense enthusiasm for life. He'd always considered himself to be a young man—aggressive, outgoing, vital.

Jennifer made him feel all of those things as though they were characteristics she'd discovered on the shelf, dusted off, and handed back to him.

"Did you join the air force to see the world?"

He looked up to discover she'd finished her dinner. Time was flying. He pushed his nearly empty plate aside and shrugged. "I'd rather talk about you."

"We've talked about me all through dinner. It's your turn." Her expression turned wary. "Or is there a Mrs. Colonel that you don't want me to know about, Colonel?"

"Matt," he said automatically.

She just stared at him.

"There's no one waiting for me at home," he said. "There never has been. I wouldn't be here, with you, if there was."

She brightened immediately. "I'm glad. I'm having too much fun to have it all spoiled now."

Innocent. How could she possibly know he was telling the truth? Matt had known men who'd used the same words with less honesty backing them up. He wanted to caution her about those men, teach her the basic tenets of survival in the world of men and women, but realized it might be counterproductive. If he was convincing, she might begin to doubt him too.

He didn't want her to doubt him, not ever.

It mattered, even though he knew she'd return to Pilau and take her life in a direction away from his.

Not for the first time that night, he wondered what might have been if he'd met her somewhere besides a tiny island in the middle of the Pacific . . . and he knew that the memory of Jennifer was going to be with him for a very long time.

Five

"I joined the air force so I could fly jets," he told her over coffee. "Like most of the guys I trained with, I wanted to fly the little ones, fighters."

"So how did a fighter-pilot hopeful end up flying transports?" She stirred both cream and sugar into her coffee, then held the cup in both hands and lifted it to her mouth.

"Remember what you said about hang gliding?" She nodded, smiling. "Fighter jets are a thousand thrills a minute. After flying a couple of trainers, I decided that slowing the pace to something under Mach One might save me a few gray hairs in the long run."

Her gaze flicked to his hair. "It appears you made the right decision."

"I haven't been entirely successful. If you look close enough, you'll see more than a couple of gray hairs sprouting. After nearly twenty years of flying the line, I guess I've earned them. Playing tag with Typhoon Harry most likely precipitated at least a dozen more."

Her laughter was soft and free. Matt let it soak through him, fill him with a kind of contentment he hadn't known in a long time. She made him want to tell her everything, a curious notion because he wasn't in the habit of talking about himself.

"I think," she said, "it would take more than the threat of a few gray hairs to keep you from doing what you wanted."

"There are a couple of advantages to flying bigger jets," he admitted. "At some point during pilot training, I learned that the bigger the jet, the more fuel it could carry and thus the farther it could go."

"Around the world."

He nodded. "Fighters are pretty much stuck close to their home base. Cargo pilots are constantly on the move." He finished his coffee and pushed the cup aside. "Besides, in the C-141, I can walk around, cook a hot lunch, take a nap, and even go to the bathroom if needs must."

"All of which must make a fighter pilot green with envy."

He shook his head. "You're talking about a different breed of men altogether. Fighter jocks think that those of us in transports are little more than bus drivers, if that. I guess they figure we deserve a few perks for doing the dirty work."

She cocked her head and gave him a considering look. "Flying through a typhoon should earn you more than a couple of perks, I'd imagine."

After so many years in the air force, Matt knew better than to expect more than a pat on the back for the successful completion of the mission. And that would probably only come after the squadron commander finished yelling at him for manhandling a reluctant passenger. Matt didn't doubt that word of what had happened on Pilau would eventually work its way back to the squadron.

The waiter interrupted his musings with suggestions regarding dessert. Jennifer shook her head and asked Matt if he'd like to go for a walk instead. A short one, though, because she didn't want to impose too much on Uncle Ricky.

Considering the rewards Uncle Ricky was deriving for a few measly hours of work, Matt wasn't concerned. The waiter went off in a snit, clearly of the opinion that a walk was no substitute for the dessert cart. Matt paid the bill and took Jennifer's hand as he helped her from her chair. He was prepared for it this time, the cool fire that leaped from her palm to his, a signal of something remarkable between two people who were hardly more than acquaintances and certainly not lovers.

Prepared for it, but hardly immune. He didn't let go of her, though, not even when moving between the tables as a solid pair became awkward. It felt too good, too right.

Too much like he never wanted to let go. He was pleased to notice that she didn't seem to mind.

The rooftop terrace was flooded with moonlight, the air a soft caress that carried with it the heady scents of paradise. A cartful of orchid leis stood next to the elevator, complete with a smiling dark-haired beauty who took Matt's money and watched with a faint expression of envy as he draped the necklace of white flowers around Jennifer's neck.

"I believe tradition allows me two kisses," he said, pulling her into the elevator for a moment of privacy. When the doors shut behind them, he punched the button for the ground floor.

Jennifer cupped the lei in her hand and looked up at him, smiling with pleasure. "It's so beautiful, Matt. Thank you." The tip of her tongue swept across her lips, leaving a glistening trail of moisture, a tantalizing invitation.

"You're beautiful," he murmured, and touched his lips first to one cheek, then the other. "Those were for tradition. This is for me." Framing her face between his hands, he covered her mouth with his. She was warm and soft, as sweet as he'd anticipated. His tongue slipped between her parted lips and caressed hers. A yearning stronger than he wanted to admit built inside him, and it took every ounce of self-control that he possessed to leave the warm secrets of her mouth.

Her lashes fluttered open to reveal eyes that were clouded with a desire that seemed to have caught her by surprise. "I wondered how it would be."

"You did?" The elevator sank to a slow stop and the doors slid open. He spared a sideways glance to confirm that no one was waiting before returning his attention to Jennifer.

"Yes, I wondered," she murmured. She touched her fingertips to her mouth, then reached up to trace a single finger across his. "I do wish we had more than this one night."

"Why?"

"Because I think kissing you could get to be a habit." Her gaze tracked the sweep of her finger as it explored his lower lip. "You're quite good at it."

A low groan escaped him. He wanted to take that inquisitive finger into his mouth to taste, to suck. She'd like that, he imagined. She'd like a lot of things that he wanted to do to her. The elevator doors slid shut again, and she dropped her hand, fingering the delicate blossoms around her neck instead.

Matt slid his hands beneath the orchid lei to stroke the satiny smooth skin of her shoulders. "Shall we do it again?"

"Kiss?"

His thumbs caressed the soft hollows of her throat, then swept across the rise of her breasts. "Yes, sweet, we can start there. With a kiss."

She shuddered beneath his touch, her eyelids drifting shut as he continued his gentle massage. He bent his head and took another kiss because he couldn't not do it.

A flicker of disappointment crossed her face when he raised his head a moment later. Every emotion was so completely honest, he mused, her innocence unmarred by the scars of lovers who'd parted in anger. Whatever experiences she might have had in the past, they'd been gentle ones.

He would be gentle with her too.

"What about that walk, hmm?"

Her smile was wry. "I think that might be a wise idea."

"Personally, I'd rather walk you only as far as my room. Kissing you behind a closed door has a certain appeal to it." His gaze narrowed on the flare of excitement in her eyes. Images excited her too. He'd remember that. "But you're not ready for that yet. Are you?"

He didn't wait for her answer, punching the button to open the doors instead. She followed him willingly enough out of the elevator, but tugged him to a stop before they were halfway across the lobby. She rested her hand on his forearm and looked up at him, a troubled expression in her eyes.

"What's wrong, Jennifer?"

Her gaze shifted around the lobby, which was surprisingly busy for that time of night. He smiled when she finally looked back at him, willing her to understand that there wasn't anything she couldn't say to him.

"I don't do one-night stands," she said in a low voice that only he could hear.

"I know you don't." He patted her hand and urged her toward the door. "Did I happen to mention that I live very close to Seattle?"

She almost stumbled, and he slipped an arm around her waist and pulled her into his side. "My home is near Tacoma. It's not more than thirty or forty miles from Seattle."

They stepped through the automatic doors, out into the tropical night, and turned left because almost everyone else was going the other way. Her silence was a curious curtain between them—and a blow to his confidence, because he'd assumed she'd greet the news with enthusiasm.

Her innocence. His arrogance. He should have known better.

He measured his steps to hers, guiding her along the broad sidewalk until they had shed the crowds and were alone on a grassy verge beneath the towering palms. He slowed the pace and brought her around to face him, his hands resting lightly on her hips.

"You're mashing my ego into the ground, sweet." He tilted up her chin with his knuckles. "I've enjoyed your company tonight. I could have sworn you felt the same."

There was a wistful expression in her gaze as she looked at him. "We won't be in Seattle very long, Colonel."

"Matt. And what does that have to do with it?"

"Matt." A tremulous sigh escaped her lips. "One night . . . dinner . . . I thought I could handle that. But more?" She shook her head as if to dispel the contradictions in her mind. "I'm not sure it's a good idea."

"Why not?" An unaccountable dread grew inside him as he felt her slipping away from him.

She regarded him seriously. "I suppose because I don't want to go back to Pilau with you on my mind."

Innocent. The word slammed him in the gut. Too innocent to tell a lie to protect her pride, too innocent to realize such an admission was tantamount to a challenge for some men.

Matt didn't want a challenge. He wanted Jennifer. How much, how long, he didn't stop to analyze.

"Would that be such a bad thing?" he murmured.

Her nod was almost imperceptible. "I suspect it might be."

"Why?"

"I've spent too many years wanting to travel, to be somewhere besides where I was." She stared into his eyes without shying away. "I'd hate to go back to Pilau and wish I was somewhere else."

I don't want to go back to Pilau with you on my mind. Matt let her words settle in a corner of his mind and knew there was nothing he could do. Jennifer was going to do this her way.

She knew where she was vulnerable, and she protected that weakness with a strength he had to admire.

He lifted a hand to caress the soft hair at her temple. "It's your life, Jennifer. You have to make the decisions that feel right to you."

"I have to admit," she said, her voice quivering, "that it doesn't feel very right, not at this moment."

He could relate to that. "Kiss me again, sweet. If one night is all I'm to have, I want—" He froze, his nerves suddenly alert to the sensation that something wasn't quite right.

It was too late.

The blow caught him behind his knees, driving him into Jennifer and down. He felt her tumble beneath him, her scream a mere whisper over his own roar of outrage. He caught his weight with his arms, trying not to crush her yet protect her in the only way he could. Out of the corner of his eye, he glimpsed a slight figure dressed in black and carrying a club of some sort. He covered Jennifer's head with his arms, knowing that he couldn't do a thing about the threat as long as she was with him.

His legs were numb one second and on fire the next, and all he could do was watch as their attacker bent down and took something from the grass. Jennifer's purse, he guessed. He would have thrown out his wallet on command when he realized that Jennifer was fighting him too. It was so unexpected, she'd squirmed out from under him before he could stop her.

His hand clutched air, but she was already in pursuit of their attacker. "Get back here, Jennifer!"

"He's got my purse!" she shouted back without breaking stride. She'd slipped off her high-heeled sandals and was fairly skimming across the grass.

"For God's sake, Jennifer, let him take it!" Matt struggled to his knees, ignoring the agony as he bellowed at the top of his lungs for her to stop. Thirty yards away, she obeyed . . . because the mugger had stopped first.

Horrified, Matt watched as the mugger raised his club. In that split second, Matt was consumed with terror. He staggered to his feet and was stumbling toward them when Jennifer landed the first blow.

With a whirling kick that resembled something out of a martial-arts movie, she knocked the club clean out of his hands. Before the mugger could recover from his surprise, she launched another kick that caught him in his stomach and laid him flat.

Matt willed his legs not to fail him as he got near enough to see Jennifer bend over the still, prone shape and pluck her glittering sequined bag from where it had fallen. Then she was hurrying back to meet him.

Figuring he'd been about as much help to her as she'd needed—none, to be absolutely blunt—Matt succumbed to the sharp, shooting pains in his legs and collapsed against the trunk of a handy palm.

He'd never get over it, not if he lived to be a hundred. The sight of Jennifer standing helplessly before the mugger, followed by her efficient handling of the situation had taken ten years off his life. Learning afterward that she had a black belt in karate wouldn't stop the gray hairs. He was convinced there would be hundreds of them come morning.

"It will be your fault," he ground out between imprecations, throwing his coat over her shoulders. The bodice of her gown had ripped at some point— probably when he fell on her—and it was practically half off her. The orchid lei was in worse shape, the delicate petals bruised and torn.

It might have been Jennifer who was bruised and torn.

He scowled to cover his rage. "When I wake up in the morning looking like my grandfather, I'll know who to blame." Her hair was caught under the collar of his coat, the simple upsweep he'd admired earlier reduced to an uncombed tangle. He freed the silky waves and brushed a couple of errant curls from her forehead.

She looked like she'd been in a brawl.

"Are we back to that 'I'm too old for you' crap, Colonel?" she demanded, hands on hips and looking like she was ready to take him on if he didn't straighten up his act.

He expelled a harsh breath. "It's Matt, Jennifer. Get it straight."

"Okay, Matt," she said sweetly. "You quit whining about your age and I'll try to remember your name."

He gritted his teeth. She was lucky he didn't spank her.

It occurred to him that she could easily return the swat and worse if the notion struck her. "Fine," he barked.

"Fine." She grinned and tucked her shoulder under his arm to help him back to the sidewalk.

By the time the stabbing agony in his legs had been reduced to occasional piercing twinges, he'd let Jennifer know in no uncertain terms that she was never to do that again. It had been foolhardy, irresponsible, and just plain stupid, he told her in a voice that she protested was much too loud.

The mugger recovered enough to slither off into the night somewhere between "No, dammit, I don't need a doctor" and "The least you could have done was tie him up so you could haul his carcass down to the police."

"You really want to spend the next few hours in the police station filing a complaint?" she asked, the disbelief patent in her voice.

He really wanted to catch the little bastard himself and teach him what happened to people who used clubs on other people. Then again, it might be more effective to let Jennifer do it.

He deserved a few lashes himself for being so careless. "I should have known better than to leave the crowds. Honolulu is a big city, paradise or no. People get mugged here just like they do in New York."

"We weren't in the mood for crowds," she said simply as they paused where she'd kicked off her sandals. She scooped them up in one hand and resumed her position beside him. "Do you feel emasculated because I acted when you couldn't?"

She didn't know, he realized. His horror at the thought of her being hurt was such a personal thing, reaching much deeper than it should, touching him in places that were still raw and hurting.

He tightened his arm around her shoulders. "No, sweet. It just scared me half to death."

"It scared me a little too." He felt a shudder move through her.

"It didn't show."

They avoided the front lobby of the hotel and found a side entrance where his grass-stained trousers and her ripped dress went unremarked. As they rode up to her room in the elevator, she asked again about his legs and he reassured her they were fine.

Sore, he admitted, but nothing a hot bath wouldn't ease. They were at the door to her room before he knew it.

"This was not the way I planned to end the evening," he said, smoothing his knuckles up and down the lapels of his coat. He could feel the contours of her body beneath the cashmere, was so tempted to push the coat aside and feel the satin of her skin . . . one last time.

"Did you figure we'd end up in your bed?" she asked with what he knew now was her customary candor.

"Not even *my* arrogance took that much for granted." He drew in a deep breath and let it out slowly. "Actually, I'd hoped we could walk down to the beach, share some laughs, some kisses . . . and make plans for seeing each other again in Seattle."

"Kind of disappointing for you all around, wasn't it?"

He shook his head. "No, Jennifer. I think I'll probably remember this night for a very long time."

"Me too." She swallowed hard and stared up at him, her eyes strangely moist. It tore at his soul to know that this was their last moment together.

"How can you look so soft and innocent and helpless?" he asked.

"I'm not exactly helpless," she said with a forced laugh.

He just stared at her.

"I'm not innocent, either."

"Maybe not in your book." He touched her lips with his thumb. "But you're soft, Jennifer. I think I've never known a woman so soft."

Her bottom lip trembled, and he knew he had to kiss her again or go mad. He cupped her chin in his fingers, leaned down, and whispered, "Let's try this one last time, sweet."

His mouth covered hers. She opened to his questing tongue, her hands reaching up and locking behind his neck as he thrust inside her. It was hot and wild, a mating of the only kind they would ever have. He devoured her softness, absorbed her taste, and lost himself in her response.

One kiss followed another. He clutched the jacket lapels, his knuckles digging into the cushion of her breasts. Their heat soaked into him, taunting him because he wanted so very badly to cup them in his palms, to caress her in ways that would drive her wild.

He couldn't, though. If he touched her, really touched her, he'd never stop.

Her ragged breaths penetrated the passionate fog gripping him, and he eased from her with a reluctance he didn't bother to hide. He took a scrap of paper from his wallet and wrote his telephone number on it.

"Call." He put it in her palm and folded her fingers over it. "If you change your mind."

Her eyes misted with regret. "Matt, I can't. I think you understand why."

The trouble was, he did.

Six

The February morning had already lost its freshness by the time Matt pulled into his garage. They'd landed at dawn, but it had taken two hours to debrief the mission. Two *agonizing* hours, because they'd already worked a twenty-hour day after only minimal crew rest.

Levering himself out of his low-slung Jaguar, he grabbed the bag that held his clothes from the passenger seat. He skirted the four-wheel-drive Jeep that was parked in the next slot, let himself into the house, and dropped his bag on the kitchen floor.

Without breaking stride, he went to the telephone answering machine and punched the button for messages. There were a half dozen, and his heart thudded painfully as he listened.

One was from the dentist, reminding him of an appointment two days ago. Matt winced because he'd forgotten to cancel it before he left. Military dentists were worse than their civilian counterparts when it came to missed appointments, and Matt knew he could look forward to a lecture from the tech sergeant when he called to reschedule.

He hit the button again. There were two messages from a friend who'd wanted to know if he'd like to go skiing, one from a neighbor wondering if he could borrow Matt's circular saw, and two from his sister

Maggie, telling him to call when he got back because she had some special news. He grinned and wondered how she'd managed to get pregnant so quickly.

Of course, she could always be calling about something else—the book she was writing, for one. But he knew better. The breathless excitement of the first message followed by the outright impatience of the next added up to an exciting event indeed. He'd bet a tenner she was pregnant.

His smile faded as he rewound the tape. Nothing from Jennifer. It had been over three weeks since they'd parted ways in Hawaii, and he hadn't heard a word from her. But then, she'd told him she wouldn't call.

He just hadn't wanted to believe it.

He turned away from the machine and climbed the stairs to his bedroom. Crossing the room, he pulled the drapes shut across the wide windows that looked out over the water, then sat down on the edge of the king-sized bed to unlace his boots. After tossing them in the general direction of the closet, he peeled off his flight suit and everything beneath it. Out of habit, he picked up the dirty clothes and dumped them into the hamper in the bathroom, knowing that if he didn't, no one else would. The price of living alone, he thought as he turned on the shower and waited for the water to warm. No one to pick up after you.

Matt stepped into the oversized shower stall and slid the glass doors shut. Ducking under the stinging spray, he wondered why he was paying attention to things like picking up after himself. It wasn't as though it was a new thing. He'd been living alone, more or less, for over twenty years.

He just noticed it more now than before.

"You're tired, Matt," he said aloud as he grabbed the soap and began working up a lather. "It's been a rugged couple of days and you're just wishing there was someone here to smooth off the rough edges."

Someone like Jennifer.

He grabbed the shampoo and worked some into

his hair, then stood under the spray until the water ran clear. Slamming his palm down on the shut-off switch, he wiped the water from his eyes, then snagged a towel from the rack. He dried himself quickly and wandered back into the bedroom. A yawn overtook him as he stood in the middle of the room, and he stretched his arms over his head in an attempt to relieve his tense muscles.

His gaze flicked over the simple, masculine furnishings, and he pictured Jennifer sprawled upon the bed—her hair a splash of color against the white sheets, her lips parted by quick, nervous breaths, her tanned body arching uninhibitedly beneath his touch.

Making love to Jennifer was fast becoming an addiction. He'd never had to settle for an imaginary sex life before, but then, he'd never wanted a woman like he wanted Jennifer.

He didn't fight the fantasies, because they were all he'd ever have of her.

So he stood erect and hurting as his body reacted to his imagination, his eyes blind to everything but those visions of a redheaded woman opening herself beneath him.

Her small breasts were swollen, the nipples hard beneath his mouth. His hand swept down her flat belly and beyond, stroking her wet heat until he felt the beginning of her tremors. He slid into her then, slowly because she was so small, so incredibly tight.

He looked down into eyes that were clouded in passion, and knew that her pleasure equaled his. Her mouth trembled, bells rang in his ears as he—

His eyes flew open. The telephone rang again. He couldn't move, not easily. His body shuddered through the fourth ring, then he willed himself to cross to the bedside table and pick up the receiver before the machine downstairs intervened.

His voice was a gruff reflection of the strain of switching gears. "Yeah?"

Silence for a moment, then, "Matt?"

It was her! His fingers flexed tighter around the

instrument, knuckles fading to white under the force of his grip. "Jennifer. Where are you?"

"You sound like I interrupted something."

"Don't worry about it. Where are you?" he asked again.

"I *knew* I should have called later," she said. "They told me at the squadron you'd just come in from a trip."

"Why'd you need to call the squadron? I gave you my number for a reason."

"Keith ate it. The man who lives next door to the kids' aunt—his name is John Allen and he flies for the other C-141 squadron. Anyway, he convinced the sergeant over at the Eighth Squadron to give me your number."

"Nice of him to take the trouble," he said, trying to put a face to the name and failing. There were a lot of pilots at McChord, some married, others not. It wouldn't make any difference, though. As far as Matt was concerned, Allen's help was no longer required.

"I thought I'd catch you before you made it to bed," she went on, "but you were probably already sound asleep."

"Never mind about that—"

"I *knew* it," she interrupted, and he could hear the dismay in her voice. "You sounded so cross when you answered. I would be, too, if I'd just got to sleep. Why don't you hang up and I'll call back later—"

It was his turn to interrupt. "I wasn't asleep."

"Everyone says that when someone wakes them up, but I've never figured out why. Is it because we feel guilty when we're caught sleeping?"

He took a deep breath and counted to three. "I'm too tired to make up stories, Jennifer. I wasn't asleep."

"*I* never pretend, of course," she said across his protest. "Everyone knows when I'm asleep. Total incoherence is hard to hide."

"Everyone?" He didn't like the sound of that. "Define everyone."

"You're not too coherent yourself. I *knew* I should

have waited to call later, but I needed to ask you a favor. Never mind about that now, though. It can wait another day."

He kicked himself for telling her he was tired. "You know I'll do whatever I can. Tell me what you need, Jennifer."

"Will you be home later this afternoon?" she asked anxiously. Clearly, she wasn't listening. "I can try to call you then, after I get back."

"Back from where?" he demanded.

"I'll tell you about that when I call. Why don't you go to bed now and get some rest."

He was losing her. "Don't be silly—"

"'Night, Matt. Sleep well."

"Don't hang—" There was a click and the phone went dead. "Up." He stood there and stared at the phone as if he could will it to ring again. It didn't, and he finally replaced the receiver.

She'd hung up on him. He was going to have to teach her not to do that.

She was going to call back, though. Knowing that stemmed his frustration and made him believe it would be possible to sleep after all. He set his alarm clock for early afternoon, then crawled between the cool sheets, folded his arms behind his head, and stared up at the ceiling as he made a mental list of the things he'd ask her when she called back.

First, he wanted a number where he could reach her. He'd let her get away from him once without leaving a trace. It wouldn't happen again.

Second, he'd ask if she would see him that night. He didn't intend to take no for an answer. He would drive to Seattle and bring her back there, where they would talk without interruptions. That was a lot of driving simply for privacy, but he didn't mind. Besides, he wanted her to see his home.

Third, he would . . . A compelling lassitude overtook Matt as the lack of sleep caught up with him.

Jennifer had called, and would call again.

It gave him a peace of mind that had been lacking for three long weeks.

He slept.

Matt bounded out of bed with the first buzz of the alarm. After a quick shower, he pulled on jeans and a long-sleeved polo shirt before running downstairs to retrieve his suitcase. It took five minutes to unpack and stash the bag in his closet. After sliding his feet into his favorite loafers, he flicked the quilt over the pillows and headed back downstairs.

By three o'clock, he'd gone through the house and made it presentable for company. Most of his effort was spent in the large, airy living room with its rattan furniture and Polynesian wall hangings. He fluffed the brightly flowered cushion of the papa-san chair, digging into the deep folds for loose change and the miscellaneous garbage that always seemed to collect there. It was his favorite place to sit when he was in that room, and he'd placed it in front of the wide expanse of windows so he could take advantage of both the view and whatever sunshine managed to break through the clouds. With brass drums for side tables and a footstool made of horsehair and antlers, it was as comfortable as a man could ask.

He pulled a tweed-covered armchair from its place by the fireplace and positioned it beside the papa-san chair. Not a great match, he admitted, but about the right size for Jennifer. For a side table, it was a toss-up between a brightly painted ceramic elephant and the teak table that was leaning into the end of the plush leather sofa. He chose the elephant because he wasn't certain the legs on the table wouldn't come off when he lifted it.

He stood back and admired his handiwork. Perfect. From there, he and Jennifer could enjoy the sunset. Tonight's promised to be spectacular, thanks to the slight haze that hung over the distant mountains. The house backed onto the water, a piece of Puget Sound for his backyard. There was room for a garden out there, as well as a decent-sized lawn, but he'd only been there a year and hadn't had time to do more than install a hot tub and pull a few of the taller weeds. The property ran all the way down to the lake, an acre or so of choice land that he'd bought years earlier when prices were low. The house he'd had built on it just last year was much too big for a bachelor, but then, he'd always figured he'd eventually marry and bring his bride there to live.

Jennifer. Impossible, of course, but he still wanted her to see it. His gaze narrowed on the weeds that seemed to be taking over the supposed garden, and he wondered if he should take the time to do a little cleanup. Or more appropriately, a big one.

He rejected the idea as soon as it surfaced, convincing himself that he wouldn't have time to make more than a dent in the task.

Maybe tomorrow. He shrugged, knowing it would take a lot more than a couple of weeds to motivate him. Gardening wasn't his forte. In fact, he'd been meaning to hire someone to take care of it, but he'd put off that chore because it was useless to do even that until he'd had the whole yard properly landscaped.

He shook off the tendrils of guilt at letting things get so far out of control and brought his thoughts back to the interior.

Matt shifted the sofa to make up for the vacancy left by the chair he'd moved to the windows, then realigned the brass-topped coffee table he'd found the year before in Korea. From the den, he brought a tall vase of peacock feathers and put it where the elephant had stood on the hearth.

Satisfied with his efforts, he went into the kitchen and checked the contents of the refrigerator. Beer, various condiments, and ice cream. A substantial selection by his usual standards, but hardly what he could offer Jennifer. He checked his watch. Three-thirty. He didn't dare make a run to the store. She might call and he couldn't take the chance of missing it.

From a cabinet above the stove, he found a pouch of Microwave popcorn next to a six-pack of Gatorade. Lunch.

Four o'clock. Matt went into the den and straightened the various framed certificates, awards, and airplane photos that covered the walls. Outdated magazines were tossed onto a tall pile of newspapers he'd been collecting to recycle. He ran his fingers along the front edge of the bookshelves, scowling at the clean swath that was left behind. A tad dusty, he admitted, although he couldn't imagine why because he'd just cleaned in there last month.

He wiped the rest of the shelf with his bare hand and reminded himself to keep the lights low so she wouldn't notice.

He didn't want her to think he was a slob.

Four-thirty. Rush hour would be under way by now. He hoped she didn't get caught up in it. Traffic in Seattle was as bad as any other metropolitan area, and she wouldn't know which areas to avoid if she was out driving around.

He could have told her if she hadn't hung up on him.

He unloaded the rest of his bags from the car and dumped them in the utility room.

He gathered up the dirty laundry and wet towels from his bathroom and shoved the whole pile into the washer. Matt didn't believe in sorting. If it couldn't be dry-cleaned, then it would have to take its chances.

The telephone rang as he was putting soap into the machine. He tripped over the flight bags but still managed to scramble to his feet and reach the phone in the kitchen before it rang a third time.

"Hello, Jennifer." Ten minutes past five o'clock. It had been a long wait.

"And hello to you, big brother. Who's Jennifer and why haven't you told me about her?" Maggie's voice held a note of amusement that would have raised a responding chuckle from Matt had he not been so disappointed.

He said hello and wondered how he could cut this short without alienating his only sister. It occurred to him that answering questions about Jennifer would only prolong the conversation, so he launched a counterattack. "What's so important that you have to tie up my answering machine with repeated calls?"

"Two calls, Matt," she said smartly. "And I wouldn't have tried a third time if I didn't remember how bad you are at returning them."

"That doesn't answer my question," he said. "What's up?"

"I'm pregnant. We just found out last week."

A well of emotion blossomed deep inside, and his impatience was tempered by his joy for his sister. "Should I ask when the baby's due?"

She laughed, obviously unembarrassed by the question. "Probably not."

He found himself laughing along with her, relieved because the subject of children hadn't always been so joyful. Maggie had miscarried her first baby months before she'd finally married the man who had helped create the child. The experience had been devastating, but they'd come to grips with the loss together. Discovering that she was pregnant again, and likely due to deliver less than nine months after the wedding, wasn't a colossal surprise. In fact, Matt couldn't have been more pleased for Will and Maggie. They'd worked hard to find their place together, and they deserved every bit of happiness that came their way.

They chatted about her health and Will's zealous attention to her well-being until Matt noticed the time and abruptly said good-bye.

Five-thirty. Where was she?

He went back into the laundry room and started up the machine. Then he wandered through the house to the front door, opening it and picking up the half-dozen newspapers that had accumulated in his absence. He sorted through them, saving that morning's edition and tossing the rest into the den on his way to the living room. Jennifer wouldn't get there for sunset. In fact, if she didn't call soon, there wouldn't be enough time to bring her back there at all.

How much time did she have before she returned to Pilau? he wondered as he eased into the papa-san chair. And what kind of advice did she need? He snapped open the newspaper and tried to concentrate.

His success was marginal. After twenty minutes without getting past the front page, he tossed it aside and stared moodily out the window. Sunset was a done deed, and the sky darkened with the coming night.

Six o'clock. What was keeping her?

He went into the den and switched on the television. From an old leather chair he'd found at a flea market, he watched the national news. Thirty minutes later, he'd absorbed nothing but fleeting news clips interspersed with images of Jennifer. As the next show began he considered calling mission control over at the Fourth Squadron and looking up this John Allen character. He was a neighbor, she'd told him. Allen could tell him Jennifer's number.

Why hadn't he thought of that before?

He surged to his feet and ran to the kitchen, where he pulled out the base directory. It occurred to him that he could just get Jennifer's address and leave for Seattle as soon as he tracked down Allen.

The telephone rang under his hand, and his stomach reacted as though he'd hit an air pocket. He let it ring twice, needing the precious seconds to restore his equilibrium.

When he said hello, he made an effort to sound casual.

"Matt," the husky voice breathed. "It's Jennifer."

As if it could be anyone else. No one, but no one, made his nerves jangle like she did by just saying his name.

He took a deep breath and asked for her telephone number. "It'll save me a lot of trouble if you decide to hang up again before we're finished talking."

An abrupt chuckle was his reward for directness. "I didn't hang up on you. I just retreated in the face of embarrassment. I'm so sorry I woke you up this morning."

"Forget it." He didn't think he should explain that she'd interrupted a fantasy who's only affiliation with sleep was the bed. "Give me your number."

She recited it, and he wrote it on the back of the base directory. They repeated the procedure with her address, which he was pleased to note was on the south end of Seattle, hardly forty minutes in good traffic.

"I can be there by seven." Real cool, Matt, he chided himself. Don't even bother to ask if she wants to see you. Just barge in and tell her what you want.

She hesitated only slightly before replying. "You don't have to drive all this way, Matt. I don't want to be a bother, really. I just wanted to get your advice on a couple of things and—"

"Jennifer," he cut in, "you knew I'd want to see you again if you called. I made that clear in Hawaii."

This time, there was a definite pause. "I never thought I'd call," she finally said. "It didn't make any sense, not then."

"What's changed?"

"I've lost my job, Matt. It looks like I won't be going back to Pilau after all."

Seven

He took her to dinner in Seattle because she wanted to get a good night's sleep before resuming her job hunt the next day. They went to a quiet seafood restaurant where they ordered the fresh catch of the day. It took less effort than reading the menu, and besides, neither of them really cared what they ate.

Matt thought Jennifer looked like she was going to drop from exhaustion—more so now than when he'd flown her off Pilau. It was hard to believe this was the same woman who had cavalierly shrugged off the mugger in Hawaii. The indomitable spirit he'd admired was so subdued as to be practically nonexistent.

The abrupt end to her dream had taken its toll.

He held her hand, his thumb rubbing over her knuckles, as he gently quizzed her about her job search.

"I've been looking for a week now," she said, "but it seems like I'm in the wrong place at the wrong time. The only openings in day-care centers are for part-time workers, and I can't afford that. I've also checked out a couple of advertisements for in-home nannies, but they're always filled by the time I call. A couple of day-care centers took my application just in case something full-time comes up, but they really didn't hold out much hope—especially when my references were so skimpy."

"What's wrong with your references?"

"That's the favor I wanted to ask you. You see, except for Keith and Carrie's aunt, there's no one local who can swear I'm not an escaped child molester." She gave a crooked smile, then glanced away as if she were embarrassed about something. "I was kind of hoping you'd let me use you for a personal reference."

"Done." He wished she knew him well enough not to have had to ask. Having one more name might have helped the job search. "What do you want? A letter? Can I call the places where you've already applied?"

She shook her head and seemed to notice for the first time that he was holding her hand. Her gaze slid back to meet his, and he could have sworn she looked less anxious than before. "I'll call them tomorrow with your name, thanks. I suppose they'll call you if they have a reason to. In the meantime, I'll keep looking."

"What happened with Keith and Carrie?" He hadn't seen the little monsters when he picked Jennifer up because she'd been waiting for him at the curb.

"I guess you could blame it on the typhoon," she said, smiling wryly. "If it weren't for Harry, we wouldn't have come to Seattle at all and I'd still have a job."

"Harry got you fired?"

She took a sip from her glass of soda water before replying. "I didn't so much get fired as replaced. Keith and Carrie's aunt Catherine has decided she wants to go back to Pilau with the kids."

"What brought that on?"

"My own fault, really. I couldn't stop talking about how beautiful the island is. After two weeks of listening to me babble about the food and sunshine and whatnot, she couldn't stand it anymore." Her eyebrows arched in mocking amusement. "I should have realized that Seattle's soggy climate wasn't on her list of favorite things. Apparently, Catherine only moved here last year and still hasn't managed to get used to the weeks of unending rain and clouds."

"It's the rainy days that make the sunshine all the more glorious when it finally breaks through," he said, holding her gaze with a promise in his own. "If she thought this climate was all rain and clouds, then she wasn't giving it a chance."

"I don't mind the rain," Jennifer said. "In fact, if I had a better wardrobe, I think I'd kind of like it. I've always imagined this is what England's like."

His gaze stroked over the soft pink sweater that she wore over indigo jeans. "I think what you've got is pretty spectacular."

She glanced down and gave a small laugh. "Wait until you've seen it twelve times in a row. Then you'll see what I mean."

Personally, he didn't care what she wore as long as she meant what she said—that she'd see him again and again and again.

She sighed and continued. "Anyway, the arrangements for Catherine to go back with the kids were made almost before I knew what was going on."

"Didn't you have a contract of some sort?"

She dipped a piece of the shrimp appetizer into a bowl of sauce and nibbled on it without much interest. "Sure. Keith and Carrie's parents gave me two months' pay in lieu of notice, which is twice what's required. And they're going to ship my clothes and other things back by airfreight, although what good the clothes will do me here, I can't imagine. Shorts and bikinis aren't exactly in season, are they? I've sent for the winter clothes I left in Montana, though. They should be here any day."

"These people strand you in Seattle and all they can give you is a couple months' pay?" he asked incredulously. "They have a lot of nerve."

A hint of a blush colored her cheeks. "Actually, they're being quite generous. Really they are. They offered me a plane ticket to anywhere in the continental United States. It was my choice to stay in the area."

Her choice. "Why?"

She avoided his gaze, staring at their joined hands instead. A tiny smile touched the corner's of her lips. "The same reason Catherine is going to Pilau, I expect. You made the Pacific Northwest sound just about irresistible."

"That's all?" he asked quietly.

She lifted her lashes and studied him for a long moment. "No, Matt, that's not all. But it's all you're going to get me to admit tonight."

He nodded, not trusting himself to speak.

"A few months, maybe a year," she said. "I've got too much to do, too many places to go to stick around here any longer than that."

"I know." It was more than he'd dreamed, months instead of moments. "I'm glad you changed your mind about wanting to see me."

Her gaze was direct and unguarded. "I didn't change my mind about *wanting* to see you. That was never the point."

"Then what did change?"

"Tactics. I realized it was already too late to just put you out of my mind because I wanted to." She took a deep breath and let it out slowly. "When I leave, it will be when something is over between us . . . not before it's even begun."

"You think we can finish what we started?" he asked softly.

"I hope so." Without seeming to do it intentionally, she slipped her hand from his and leaned back into the cushions of the booth. He noticed, but let her get away with it.

For now.

Her fingers toyed with the cowl neckline of her sweater, and he wondered how much money she'd had to spend just to have enough clothes to keep herself warm. The typhoon refugees they'd boarded on Pilau hadn't been allowed luggage. There hadn't been time to load it and get away safely. She'd even had to buy a dress just to go out to dinner with him that night in Hawaii, and as far as he knew, that was ruined.

He polished off the shrimp, then said, "My sister has left a few odds and ends at my place over the years. She's about your size, maybe a bit taller. I could bring them by tomorrow if you like."

She looked surprised at his offer, then surprised him by accepting. "I'd like that. Catherine let me use what I could of hers, but not many of her things fit."

"It's a deal. Call me when you get back from job hunting and I'll drop by."

"Why don't you let me come after them?" she asked. "It's not fair making you drive all over the Puget Sound when I'm perfectly capable of doing my share."

He shook his head. He wanted her in his home more than he wanted to breathe, but not that way. If the exhaustion she was exhibiting tonight was anything to go by, he didn't want her out on the dark roads by herself after another long day.

"I'll do it, Jennifer." He caught her gaze with his and dared her to argue.

Revealing a sensible streak, she didn't, and he nodded with satisfaction.

"So where are you looking for a job?"

She laughed weakly. "Anywhere I can find one. I've been from one end of Seattle to the other in the last week. Catherine was kind enough to lend me her car, so I've been able to get around without much hassle."

It was the least she could do, he figured. "Have you considered looking a little bit farther south?"

"How far south?"

He kept his expression carefully neutral. "More toward the Tacoma area, I guess. It's worth a try, especially since you haven't had any luck in Seattle."

She cocked her head and considered it. "It couldn't hurt to look. I'll pick up a Tacoma paper tomorrow and check the listings."

A victory of sorts, he thought. Now all he could do

was hope she found something. There was the other possibility she hadn't mentioned, though. "What about the organization that found you the job on Pilau? Have you considered getting in touch with them?"

"Of course I did."

She was drawing circles on the tablecloth with her finger and didn't notice his scowl. It wasn't the answer he'd wanted to hear. When she looked up from her invisible doodle, it struck him that she wasn't altogether comfortable about something. If it weren't for the fact that he didn't know her well enough to judge, he'd swear she was about to tell a lie.

That idea flickered in his mind, then was extinguished by the sheer absurdity of it. What reason would Jennifer have to lie about something like this? He kicked his imagination where it hurt and concentrated on what she was saying.

"I let them know I was available a week ago. But last time, it took three months for the right job to come up and two more before all the arrangements were made for me to go. I figure it will take at least that long this time."

He hadn't realized he'd been holding his breath until it suddenly whooshed out and made the candle's flame dance wildly. Five months, give or take.

Perhaps he'd have gotten her out of his system by then, and could get on with his life without needing this aspiring globe-trotter at his side.

The waitress arrived with dinner, and Matt pretended to be absorbed in his food so as to encourage Jennifer to eat. She didn't look like she'd taken time for a real meal since he'd seen her last. Either his strategy worked or she was hungry enough not to notice his silence, because she polished off the grouper steak and rice just moments after he finished his own.

"How much longer are you going to stay with the aunt?" he asked after the waitress removed their plates.

"Until I get a job and can get relocated. Or until they pack up for Pilau. Whichever comes first."

"When do they leave?"

"A couple of weeks, I think. Catherine has a lot of organizing to do."

His gaze sharpened on her, but she gave no hint of the alarm she had to be feeling. She was in a strange place, without a job or a car or a place to live.

"Jennifer?"

"Hmm?" She looked at him over the rim of her coffee cup.

"Are you okay for money?"

He was relieved that she didn't take offense. She just smiled and said, "Money isn't what I'm worried about, Matt. It's being adrift, not having an anchor, I guess, that's making me crazy."

"You've got me."

"That's not what I meant." She put her cup down and folded her hands in front of it. "I've always had responsibilities, people who relied on me. I'm finding it difficult to adjust to the fact that the only thing I have to do each morning is begin rebuilding my life at every level."

"Finding a job will make you feel more secure?"

"I hope so."

Two weeks. He wondered what kind of toll the days would take on her if she didn't find a job. He made a mental note to call the squadron scheduler to ensure he didn't get sent out on a trip anytime soon.

"You've had a rough week, honey. I wish I could have been here for you."

"Moral support counts for more than you can imagine."

"So why do you still look like a whipped puppy?"

"Every time we're together, I've been horribly exhausted for one reason or another." Her expression was tinged with regret. "I wish you could have known me first in my strong moments, not my weak ones."

He studied her for a long moment before replying.

"Everyone gets thrown for a loop now and then. You're handling it more gracefully than most."

A glimmer of a smile brightened her face. "You've succeeded in making me feel better, I think." A giant yawn overtook her, and he smiled as she tried to fight it and failed.

She was determined, though, to stay the course. "Do you realize we've spent yet another dinner talking about me? Here I am, rambling on about my problems, and you're probably still exhausted from your trip."

"I'm not the one who's yawning," he pointed out. "I'll take you home as soon as you've finished your coffee so you can get some rest."

"I'm not leaving until you tell me about the exciting places you've been in the last three weeks."

For the first time all night, her eyes took on their familiar sparkle. Jennifer wasn't just being polite, he realized. She really wanted to know. The excitement and adventures that he'd begun to take for granted were as thrilling to her now as they had been to him twenty years ago.

So he told her about his whistle-stop tour of a half-dozen South and Central American countries. They'd been gone twelve days, but it had seemed like more because of all that had been packed into the mission.

Jennifer wanted to know it all. When the waitress refilled their coffee cups, Matt tried to condense his tale so that he could get Jennifer home, but she made him go back and fill in the details. They'd only made it out of Bolivia by ten o'clock, and her yawns were becoming less easy to defeat.

Matt made a command decision to wind it down, no matter how much she protested. He breezed through Panama, Honduras, and Costa Rica at the speed of light, then signaled the waitress for the check.

"And you just got back this morning?" Jennifer asked. "No wonder you sounded so grouchy when I called." She finished her coffee and pushed it aside. "You must be bushed."

He shook his head. "That was last week. The trip I got back from this morning was only three days long."

"Where to?"

"Here and there. It was classified."

Her eyes rounded with interest. "What kinds of missions are classified?"

"Secret ones."

She giggled. "In other words, that's all I get to know."

"That's about it." He threw some money on top of the check and pulled Jennifer from the booth. Retrieving their coats from the cloakroom, he buttoned Jennifer into hers before shrugging into his own. Her eyelids were drooping now, and he knew he had only minutes before she fell asleep on him.

Somehow, he wasn't bothered.

It was colder outside, the air heavy with a cloying mist that made him shiver as they left the warm restaurant. He put his arm around Jennifer and steered her towards his car. After tucking her inside, he slipped into the driver's seat and started the engine. He let it idle, waiting for the heater to kick in before putting the car into gear.

"Matt?"

"Hmm?"

"Thank you for tonight." She rolled her head on the headrest to look at him. "I'm sorry I wasn't better company."

He reached out to stroke her cheek. "If you were such a lousy date, why do I want to ask you out again tomorrow night?"

"I haven't a clue." She pressed against his hand, her eyelids drifting shut. "Are you asking?"

"I'm asking." He leaned across the console and touched his lips to her forehead. "Would you have dinner with me tomorrow?"

She turned her head and kissed the palm of his hand. "I'd like that very much."

She fell asleep before he could tell her that he'd like that very much too. He watched her for a long moment, then kissed her again.

Yes, he thought, he'd like that very much too.

He didn't even mind knowing the chances were excellent she'd end the evening much as she'd ended this one—by falling asleep on him.

For the next three nights, Matt drove to Seattle and took Jennifer to restaurants that were easy drives from Catherine's home. Jennifer would talk only in general terms about her job search, claiming that recounting her lack of progress increased her frustration. Matt knew only that she was looking both in Seattle and Tacoma, and that if she didn't find a day-care job soon, she was going to consider something along the lines of waiting tables or clerking in a shop. Either of those would be more financially rewarding than taking care of kids, she admitted, and at least as grueling, if not more so.

She wanted to work with kids, though, and was determined to keep up the search as long as she could afford to. Without telling her, Matt called all his married friends and asked them if they'd heard of anything in the area. Nothing had surfaced yet, but he figured there was always a chance.

Over the course of those dinners, Matt got to know Jennifer and told her more about himself than he would have had she been anyone else. It was impossible not to, what with her insatiable curiosity about everyone and everything around her.

They were never out late, and their nightly goodbyes were chaste reflections of the quiet friendship that was growing between them. It was as if Hawaii had never happened . . . as if they'd never kissed like lovers, never shared even the smallest intimacy.

For the moment it was enough for Matt. The rest would come in its own time, when Jennifer was ready.

He could wait. Barely.

Jennifer didn't exactly go out of her way to make it easy for him. Innocently or not, she never let him forget that there was a sensual exciting woman behind the friend.

The evening he arrived a few minutes early to pick her up was a prime example.

Catherine let him inside, a remote phone in one hand. She pointed down the hall with the other. "She's bathing the kids. Why don't you go let her know you're here."

Matt followed the sounds of high-pitched squeals and splashing water to an open door. Jennifer was on her knees, bending over the edge of the tub as she alternated washing with tickling. Matt leaned against the doorjamb, enjoying her laughter and gentle coos. Up to her elbows in suds, she looked as happy as he'd ever seen her. No wonder she was so determined to get a job in child care of some sort, he mused.

She was a natural mother. An image of Jennifer, fat and sassy in pregnancy, slid across the viewfinder of his mind. A baby nursing at her breast, another tugging at her skirt.

Jennifer, with a smile on her face that was filled with the endless wonder of motherhood.

Jenny, sharing her enthusiasm for life with the lives she'd helped create.

It was a vision worth framing.

Carrie saw him first. "Kernel Matt?"

Jennifer looked over her shoulder and winced. "I'm late?"

He shook his head. "I'm early. Take your time."

Intent on not being ignored, Keith launched a high wave that crested the side of the tub and drenched Jennifer. "Why you little dickens!" she exclaimed, counterattacking with a handful of suds that she mashed onto the top of his head. The play got rough then, with water splashing all over the bathroom, suds landing in the most ridiculous places, and screams of delight filling the air. When Jennifer called a halt a few minutes later, the kids weren't the only ones who looked like they'd had a bath.

Matt tossed her a couple of towels, which she used on the kids, drying them all over before sending them giggling to their rooms with a challenge to get dressed while she cleaned up the mess. Still laughing, she dabbed at her face and arms, then dropped the towels on the floor. "I know I don't look like it, but I can be ready in fifteen minutes."

Matt hardly heard her. He was too busy staring. The front of her white blouse was soaked to the point of being nearly transparent. The material clung to her small, firm breasts, revealing not only the explicit contours of her nipples, but their darker color as well. The shade of pink roses, he thought, and wondered if they'd be darker or lighter without the translucent screen of her blouse.

As he stared the nipples hardened and pushed against her blouse. Oh Lord, but she was beautiful. He wanted to close the short distance between them and lay his palms against the thrusting nubs. His mouth. . . . A familiar, heave ache settled in his groin. He dragged his gaze from her breasts and caught the heated look of desire on her own face.

She licked her lips. "You look . . . hungry."

"I am." He took a step toward her, but she shook her head.

"I should get dressed. Catherine, the kids." She gestured weakly with one hand.

His stare went back to her nipples. "We could always skip dinner," he murmured. "My place isn't that far away."

She gave a soft cry, lifting a hand to cover one breast as she took deep, gulping breaths. Matt nearly went out of his mind as he imagined his hand beneath hers, caressing, teasing, provoking.

He wanted her now, tonight.

She shook her head again, a panicked look filling her expression. "I can't. Not tonight. I promised Catherine I'd be home early so she can go out to a late movie."

"To hell with Catherine," he growled, reaching to cover her hand with his. Her wet, sizzling heat penetrated his skin and left him shaking.

"I didn't mean to tease" she said. "But you were looking at me—"

"Like I wanted to make love with you," he finished for her, sliding his hand up to her neck and into her hair. "And you looked like you wanted the same."

Her eyes were clear and honest. "I do. But not in a hurry or on a schedule."

Her words made his heart slam against his chest. "So it's a question of when, not if."

She nodded.

He stared at her for a long moment, then let out a long, harsh breath. "Good, sweet. As long as we both know."

"We know."

The waiting became an exquisite torture. For both of them, Matt liked to think. In the meantime, there were other things to concentrate on.

Jennifer seemed to have recovered her spirit—most of it, anyway. Her eyes sparkled with enthusiasm again, although Matt wasn't always certain it was the real thing or a brave act for his benefit.

His protective instincts were fully aroused when it came to Jennifer, but she would have none of it. It was her life, and she was the one who had to put it back together, she insisted. As desperate as her situation was—or so he imagined—she allowed him to do no more than loan her his sister's clothes and take her to dinner. He had even offered to drive her around to interviews, but she'd insisted upon going alone.

He wasn't to worry, she told him every time he expressed concern about her situation. At times, she seemed more worried about him than about herself.

The sparkle might be back, he realized, but she was a different women, older, and he would have given anything to revive that youthful passion for life that had been so abundant in her before. Eventually, though, he came to realize that the passion wasn't really missing at all. Temporarily displaced, perhaps, by her determination to make her own way in the world that had spun her in an unexpected direction, but definitely not missing.

After two days' crew rest, Matt had gone back to work in the squadron. There wasn't much happening, except, as usual, there were too many trips on the schedule and too few pilots available to fill them. He dodged the system as best he could, using every trick and excuse he'd learned over his career, but finally had to surrender. Nine days after he got back, he had to leave for a five-day trip to Germany.

The night before he left, he took Jennifer to a small Italian restaurant that had better atmosphere than food, and annoyingly efficient service that made conversation a hit-or-miss proposition. He waited until they'd finished dinner and could talk without interruption before he told her about the trip.

"How long?" she asked.

"Five days." Unless the aircraft broke down, or got diverted, or any number of events that could keep him out in the system for double or even triple that time. He didn't tell her that part.

She lowered her gaze to her lap, but not before he detected something that looked like panic in her eyes. Panic? What was going on that he didn't know about?

"What's wrong, honey?"

"Nothing." She cleared her throat, and when she looked up at him, her eyes were clear and bright. "Chalk it up as envy, Colonel."

She hadn't called him Colonel since Hawaii, and he didn't like it any better now than he had then. It was as if she was trying to distance herself from him.

He needed her to believe he wasn't going voluntarily. "I tried to get out of it, but they're shorthanded at the squadron and I didn't really have a choice."

"Don't be silly." She thrust her fingers through her hair and gave him a smooth, fake smile. "If I had a chance to fly to Germany for a couple of days, I'd jump at it."

"It's not exactly a pleasure trip."

"And you're not going to work twenty-four hours a day, either." She shoved her coffee cup aside. "Too bad about the weather, though. No tennis this time of year, is there?"

He wished he knew what the hell was going on in her head. She'd pulled up every defense mechanism and had them functioning at maximum efficiency. "I'll be back before you know it."

"Of course you will." She looked like she didn't believe him. "It's probably for the best, anyway. I've been taking you for granted these last few days."

"Not so I'd notice." He reached across the table and tilted her chin up with his fingers. "I know how much your independence means to you, Jennifer, but I've been standing on the sidelines watching you struggle and I want to do more than take you to dinner. If you'll let me."

"It's my struggle."

"It doesn't have to be." He stroked the side of her face once before dropping his hand to the table between them.

"I don't want you to feel sorry for me," she said vehemently.

"And I don't want you to reject my help just because you're afraid of losing that damned independence you value so highly."

She looked as though she wanted to strangle him. "What good is it going to do me to rely on someone who's hardly ever here?"

Now just where did that come from? Matt wondered. It wasn't like she didn't know what he did for a living. He shook his head in confusion and tried to reason with her. "It's my job, Jennifer. I can't help it if I have to be gone a lot."

"Then it's a good thing I'm so independent, isn't it?" She had a smug smile on her face and he realized she imagined she'd won that point.

He just stared at her. She was determined to fight

with him, and he was warming to the hostilities with an almost detached curiosity. He knew the glimpse of panic he'd seen was at the bottom of it all. The argument was a feint to keep him from prying.

"You didn't get where you are today by relying on someone else to do it for you," she said.

"Nor did I pretend I could do it alone. There were lots of people who helped me get what I wanted out of life. I took what they offered because they were in a position to help and I knew I'd be able to do the same for others someday."

"And did you?"

"What do you think?"

She gazed blankly at him. He let that insult roll off his back because that wasn't the point he was trying to make.

He gestured toward the parking lot. "I couldn't have found the car if I hadn't told a bunch of people I was looking for an old Jaguar XJS. The property my house is built on came to my notice because I'd let people know I was in the market."

"Nobody got you your job."

He felt like beating his head against the table. "I got the job on merit. It took teamwork to get good enough to keep it."

She threw her napkin on the table and grabbed her purse. "It's late. Would you please take me home?"

He would, but only because he knew she'd walk if he didn't.

He pulled up in front of Catherine's house, and they sat in silence for a minute. In the meek glow of the porch light, shadows of exhaustion and worry played across Jennifer's face. He wanted to hold her, to comfort her and tell her everything would be all right.

She didn't look like she was in the mood to believe him. She looked fragile, as though one more straw would break her into a million pieces.

He looked away, because he knew she wouldn't want him to see her like that. Someday, perhaps, when she'd learned to trust him, she would discover that weakness could be shared too.

Like joy. And love.

"Thank you for dinner." Her voice had a slight wobble to it that he knew she must hate.

"You're welcome."

It was a positive sign that she didn't get out of the car. He gave her a minute just to make sure, then asked, "What's so awful that you can't tell me about it?" He turned sideways in his seat and hooked his arm over the steering wheel.

"Nothing." She didn't look at him, but continued to stare out the window. "I'm sorry I picked a fight."

"It's okay. It wasn't much of one anyway."

"I wouldn't blame you if you didn't want to see me again." She looked at him, her expression a cross between regret and impatience. "I don't know what got into me. One minute we were having a lovely time, and the next I was trying to make you feel guilty for leaving."

"It worked. I feel like a heel." He smiled to soften his words. "It would make me feel better if you'd tell me what's really bothering you."

The panic was back. He could feel it, amplified in the small confines of the car until it was almost a physical thing. He could almost see it, touch it, then it was gone, reabsorbed by the woman at his side who refused to share her fears.

He reached across the console and took her hand in his, cupping her cold, trembling fingers in his palm. "I suppose I'm selfish enough to hope you'll miss me while I'm gone."

She looked down at their hands, then searched his face with a thoroughness he found disconcerting. "It's madness, you know."

"What is?"

"The way you make me feel every time you touch me . . . or look at me." She raised a hand to his face and traced the line of his eyebrows with a delicacy he found wildly erotic. Desire coiled through him so fast, it left him panting.

He took a deep breath and began the battle for control. He wasn't a teenager and he wasn't going to act like one.

He was a man who desired her, and he was going to teach her how exciting that desire could be. Hot, thorough, satisfying desire.

"How do I make you feel, Jenny?" He brought her other hand beneath his jacket to his chest and let the irregular beat of his heart reassure her. "Can you tell me, baby?" Or would you rather listen to me tell you what you do to me?"

A flicker of arousal clouded her gaze. "Tell me."

Her fingers spread across his shirt, and he slid a hand behind her head to urge her closer. "Do you know that I've had fantasies about you almost nonstop since we kissed that first time in Hawaii?"

"Fantasies?" It was a breathless whisper that sent his heart beating faster.

"Yes, sweet. Awake fantasies, not dreams. I've made love to you so many times, so many ways." She was so close now, he could feel the moist warmth of her breath. His fingers found the uneven pulse at her throat and stroked it with gentle insistence.

"Even before you knew I was coming back to you?"

He liked the way she'd put that. "Fantasies were all you left me with, Jenny." He fondled the collar of her cardigan sweater, then flicked open the buttons down the center until he could see the soft rise of her breasts above the lacy cups of her bra. The heat in his groin condensed to a pinpoint of sweet, excruciating desire.

"Do you know that I haven't been able to kiss you—*really* kiss you—because I was afraid I'd lose control and scare you away?"

"I'm not afraid," she whispered.

"You should be." He looked up from her breasts. "I've wanted you in my bed for so long that I'm not going to be very gentle with you. At least, not the first time."

"You won't hurt me."

He gave a short laugh. "I'll try not to, baby. I'll try."

He turned his attention back to her breasts, wanting her mouth, too, but finding all the choices an exhilarating experience.

There were so many textures that his fantasy had left undiscovered, so many sensations unimagined.

"Just a taste, Jenny," he said roughly. "A touch. I can't go away tomorrow without something real in my head."

Her next words startled him. "We could always go to your place."

He sucked in a chestful of air and let it out slowly. "We could, sweet. But I have to report at five in the morning, and if I took you home with me, I'd end up flying that damn plane in my sleep."

"Oh."

"Rain check?" he asked, seeing the disappointment in her expression and letting it warm his ragged nerves.

She nodded.

His thumbs traced the gentle curves of her small breasts, rimming the lace once, twice . . . then again when he saw how much she liked it. Her breaths were gasps of surprise and pleasure, and the moan that escaped her lips nurtured his own excitement.

Her tongue drew a wet path across her lips, and he resisted her mouth no longer. He leaned forward until his lips were touching hers. Her mouth opened beneath his, her tongue a lazy whip that flicked across his teeth. He let her play, enjoying the teasing as she accustomed herself to his mouth. Her lips were mobile and daring beneath his, her taste a remembered joy.

He deepened the kiss as his fingers grasped her bra and tugged the lace down across her erect nipples. He swallowed her cry of pleasure and stroked her mouth with deep, rhythmic thrusts of his tongue as his thumbs toyed with the velvet-covered nubs. She clenched her hands against his chest, then they flattened as he lulled her with gentle kisses. When he lowered her mouth to suckle at her breasts, her nails sank in.

He wanted more, needed more. Jennifer's soft cries and hot kisses were driving him over the edge. Wrong time, wrong place. He cursed his luck.

Definitely, though, the right woman. Regretfully, he slipped the cups of her bra back over her wet, rosy nipples—slowly, so that not a single sensation was lost. He buttoned her sweater with hands that shook.

"You okay, sweet?" His voice shook, too, but he didn't care if she knew how vulnerable he was to her.

"No." She buried her face in his chest. "I don't want you to go."

"Tonight or on the trip tomorrow?"

"Neither."

He loved her honesty. Slipping his arms around her, he held her as their hearts flew from one erratic rhythm into another, taking their time before settling into an easier cadence.

"Jennifer?"

"Hmm?"

"The next time, I won't stop."

"The next time, I won't let you."

Eight

"We're sorry. You have reached a number that has been disconnected or is no longer in service. If you feel you have reached this recording in error, please check the number and try your call again."

He'd already done that. Catherine's telephone had been disconnected while he was in Germany. Jennifer had disappeared.

Cradling the receiver, Matt slouched back in the chair and frowned at the crew control board on the opposite wall. Aircrews were flying missions all over the world with flight plans ranging from Iceland to Australia. Yet if Matt needed to talk with a crew member for any reason, all he would have to do was check the mission orders, pick up the telephone, and track him down. If the mission had been diverted, someone would know where it had been diverted to. Or if the plane was broken and the crew was taking advantage of some unexpected time off, they were still required to check in with mission control every so often.

Even if the plane was in the air, they only had to wait for it to come down. Unless it was urgent, and then they'd rig a patch and talk over the drone of the engines.

Finding someone wasn't always fast or easy, but it

could be done. Crews couldn't be lost because there were too many people keeping track of them.

Jennifer didn't have that kind of support. That was going to make her a lot harder to find.

He understood her panic now. She'd known the night before he left for Germany that she'd have to find another place to live. But where?

If she'd only told him, he would have demanded she stay at his home while he was away . . . which was precisely why she hadn't said a word, he realized. She'd decided to go to an apartment or hotel rather than sacrifice even a smidgen of her independence by asking for help.

Jennifer's independent nature was beginning to chafe in some rather annoying places.

He picked up the telephone again. After dialing his home number, he tapped in the code for messages. Nothing from Jennifer.

Matt swung his feet off the desk and headed out the door. Five minutes later, he'd learned from Fourth Squadron mission control that John Allen had left on a mission even before Matt had and wasn't back yet. Matt thought to ask if Allen was married. No help on that count, either. Allen was single and lived alone. So much for Catherine's next-door neighbor.

Matt checked his watch. Six o'clock. He'd told her he wasn't due in until later that night. If she was going to call, she probably wouldn't do it until tomorrow.

Not good enough.

Hurrying back to the squadron, he threw his bags into his Jag and headed for Seattle—just in case the phone had been disconnected prematurely. It hadn't. He could tell without getting out of the car that the house was empty. He went up the walk and peeked in the windows just in case.

They were gone.

Matt canvassed the neighborhood, hurrying through the light rain that had begun to fall on his drive north. Keith and Carrie's aunt hadn't left her forwarding address with anyone he talked to. Most of them hadn't even seen the redheaded woman who had been living there for the past month. By the time he went back to his car, his uniform was soaked and he felt totally defeated.

Jennifer had disappeared into thin air. Again.

Matt checked his messages once more when he got home. Nothing new. But then, he really hadn't expected anything. Jennifer would call when she was ready. She had more important things to do with her life besides worry about checking in with a man who was more often gone than not.

He snagged a beer from the refrigerator and carried it into the living room, where he drank it standing up as he leafed through the week's mail. Rain pelted against the windows, obscuring stars and moon. Ignoring his damp flight suit, Matt took a moment to watch as nature performed its wet chorus.

A jagged streak of lightning lit up the night sky, outlining the spectacular view for a split second. The lake was rough with waves cut by the wind and pounded by the rain. At the lake's edge, a cluster of willows bent and flared beneath the storm's fury. Boat docks bobbled in the water, clinging to land by sheer determination, it seemed. His own dock looked as though it could manage whatever this storm threw at it and more. He'd made it strong, just like he'd designed his home. Strong and safe.

God only knew what kind of place Jennifer had found to live in. Turning his back to the windows, he gritted his teeth and decided he'd give her twenty-four hours before he started calling around to apartment houses and hotels. Grabbing his bag, he bounded up the stairs and tore off the damp uniform.

The phone rang while he was in the shower.

He slid open the glass doors and grabbed the remote from where he'd left it on the vanity. Switching it on, he moved back under the steaming water.

"It's me. Jennifer."

A shiver of relief shot through him. "Where are you?"

"I'm not going to tell you. It's a dump."

He took a second to curb his impatience before asking, "A Seattle dump or a Tacoma dump?" He didn't bother to ask how bad it was. She wouldn't be there any longer than it took him to pick her up.

"Tacoma."

"Good. At least I won't have to drive back to Seattle tonight. Can you be ready in thirty minutes?" He grabbed the soap and worked a thick lather across his chest and arms.

"I just told you, you can't come here." She sounded almost too tired to argue with him. "Why were you in Seattle?"

"To look for you, of course. It wouldn't have been necessary if you'd let me know you were moving." His voice was gruffly reprimanding, but he couldn't help it. She'd made him worry for no good reason, and he wasn't going to let her get away with it.

"Matt, you knew I was going to have to move sooner or later. Maybe I thought I was capable of finding a place on my own."

"And maybe you were afraid I wouldn't let you move into that dump," he growled, rinsing the lather from his body and shutting off the shower.

"There wasn't anything you could do to stop me."

"Don't bet on it." He squeezed the phone between his ear and shoulder and ran a towel over his body. "Now tell me where to pick you up and we'll go out for dinner."

"It's late."

"It's early."

"I have to get up early."

"Tomorrow's Sunday. You can't do anything about job hunting all day."

"I've already eaten."

"You can watch me. I had a box lunch at Norton

and nothing since." He draped the towel over the bar and pulled his spare electric razor from a drawer.

"Where's Norton?"

"Southern California. Now quit stalling and give me your address."

She hesitated just long enough for him to worry that she wasn't going to tell him. He forced a gentler note. "I want to see you, Jennifer. Please."

Her sigh was long and weary. "I'm so worn-out, Matt. Aren't you getting tired of watching me yawn through dinner?"

"No." He felt like a heel for forcing her. "It's been nearly a week, Jenny. Surely you can spare me an hour."

It seemed she could. "There's a twenty-four-hour coffee shop just a couple of blocks from here, a ten-minute walk. I'll meet you there." She gave him the address and disconnected before he could argue.

Terrific, he thought as he ran the razor over his chin. Not only was Jennifer living in a dump, she didn't have any transportation. She was going to walk through what was probably a bad neighborhood, in the dark, in the rain.

Black belt or not, he didn't like it. She was probably too tired to fight off a flea, much less a bigger threat.

He pulled on dark wool slacks, a long-sleeved shirt, and a yellow crewneck sweater. Thunder boomed overhead as he skipped down the stairs, electrical interference from the storm causing the lights to blink off and on. He shrugged into a lined, weatherproof coat and hurried out to the Jeep. What with all the water on the roads, it was the logical choice.

Besides, the Jaguar wouldn't have enough room for both Jenny and whatever baggage she might have accumulated over the past month.

He was bringing her back with him and he wasn't taking no for an answer.

She didn't even have a proper coat, was Matt's first thought when she walked into the coffee shop.

Her yellow slicker had kept the water from soaking through, but provided little protection from the cold. He ground his teeth as he hung it on a peg in the entryway, only just managing to keep from haranguing her about it because he knew she couldn't wear what she didn't have. She'd probably given back the coat Catherine had loaned her. He knew better, too, than to berate her for not buying something while she waited for her clothes from Montana to catch up with her. She'd only tell him it was her business.

Independence and all that. He had bigger battles to fight that night.

"Sorry to keep you waiting," she said. "My key got stuck in my lock and I had to borrow a pair of pliers to get it out." She grinned up at him in the dim entryway. "I had to knock on eleven doors before I found someone who both spoke English and had some tools."

She'd been knocking on strangers' doors. In a dump. At night. He couldn't stand it. His hand slipped under the fall of hair at her nape, and he backed her into a corner, shielding her from the entryway with his body. It was privacy of a sort.

She looked up at him, and he saw that the exhaustion he'd heard over the telephone had drawn dark shadows beneath her eyes. He felt a stab of guilt that she was there with him instead of in bed.

In bed in the dump where she lived. The guilt evaporated. His fingers traced the signs of her exhaustion, then threaded into her hair.

"I've missed you." He rubbed his lips across hers and felt the shuddering of her soft breasts through the layers of fabric between them.

"I've missed you too," she whispered, resting her hands on his chest. "I didn't want to, but it happened anyway."

"Open your mouth, baby," he demanded softly. "I've been thinking about how you taste for five long days. And nights. I can't wait any longer."

Her lips parted in a gasp that he swallowed with hungry impatience. His arms slipped around her, drawing her hard against his thighs as he explored her mouth with a thoroughness that only hinted at his need for her. There was nothing gentle in the kiss, yet he wasn't oblivious to the fact that she was kissing him back with an eagerness that equaled his own.

His mouth slanted over hers from one angle, then another. He felt her arms snake around his neck just moments before she sagged against him, a whimper of passion escaping her lips. Then the outside door banged open and a cold breeze preceded the sound of arriving customers. He slackened his hold on her, but didn't move away until the new arrivals had walked past them into the coffee shop.

He looked down at her mouth, which was red and swollen, and smiled. "You look like you've been kissed."

"I feel like it." Her fingertips slid over her lips. "Do you think anyone will notice?"

"They'll notice." He brushed her fingers aside and touched his thumb to her bottom lip. "Want to skip dinner and go neck in the Jeep?"

She shook her head. "Not yet. You said you were starving."

Not yet. He liked the way she said that.

"A man can be hungry for more than food," he teased, his lips tracking across the bridge of her nose.

"And a woman should be able to tell which he needs and in what order," she returned, an impish smile curving her lips. "Considering how much time we spend in restaurants, I think your priorities are pretty well set. Do you realize that about the only thing we do together is eat?"

"Which goes to show how little time we've had." He slid his arm around her waist and guided her into the restaurant. They scooted into a booth along the back wall and ordered a hamburger and fries for Matt and coffee for both of them.

While they waited he asked her about her job search, deliberately avoiding the subject of where she was living. Time enough for that later.

"I'm going to give it one more week before I start

looking for something besides child care," she said, shaking her head. "I never imagined it would be so difficult finding a job. I guess that shows an incredible arrogance on my part, because there are tons of perfectly capable people out there looking for work and not having any better luck than me. I'm beginning to feel like one of those nameless statistics you read about in the newspaper."

The coffee arrived, and she curled her fingers around the mug as though its heat was all she'd been waiting for. Matt studied her across the rim of his own cup, noticing that she looked surprisingly cheerful. Her eyes sparkled as brightly as they had that night in Hawaii, and he detected a tiny dimple at the corner of her smile.

Even with the dark circles of exhaustion beneath her eyes, he got the impression she was stronger now than he'd ever seen her. Happier. "If the job hunt is going so badly, why do you look like you're on top of the world?"

"I think being out of Catherine's is doing me some good." She loosened her grasp on the mug and poured a dollop of cream into the black liquid. She added a packet of sugar and stirred. "I miss Keith and Carrie, but it was such a strain listening to their plans and knowing I wouldn't be going back with them to Pilau."

"When did they leave?"

"Yesterday, but I moved out three days ago when the movers came to pack up Catherine's things."

He frowned. "I seem to remember your saying money wasn't a problem. Care to explain why you're living in a dump?"

"I said money wasn't a problem, not that I could afford to throw it away."

"Finding a decent place to live isn't necessarily throwing it away."

"And by careful budgeting, I can afford not to work for a year or more." She held his gaze, her own steady, determined.

She had a point. He didn't happen to like it.

"I'll find a job soon, though. I'm not worried. Not really." She took a cautious sip of her coffee and changed the subject. "I thought you weren't due back until later tonight."

"We picked up half a day on the East Coast and managed to stay ahead all the way home. We landed midafternoon."

Her brow knit in bewilderment. "How do you pick up half a day?"

"Actually, we picked it up at night." He grinned at her confusion and explained. "We're allowed so many hours of crew rest for the time we fly. Sometimes—like this trip—they allow some extra for one reason or another. The crew decided they'd rather get home early and skip the extra off-duty time." He didn't mention that it had been his idea that they press for home on a compressed schedule. The crew hadn't minded one way or another, although a couple of the enlisted men had grumbled about losing half a day's per diem.

He'd had to promise to make it up to them. The next trip, drinks would be on him.

His food came and he ate while Jennifer recounted the last days with Keith and Carrie. Their aunt apparently hadn't quite got the hang of keeping track of the pair, and most of Jennifer's free time had been spent watching them so Catherine could get ready for the trip. Not that she'd had much time to spare for the children, as far as Matt could tell. Driving from one end of the Puget Sound to the other in search of a job took most of the daylight hours and nearly all of her energy.

He ate as quickly as he could without losing too many points in the manners category and signaled for the bill. "I've had enough," he said when she looked at him in surprise. "Let's go."

She checked her watch. "Seems like I promised you an hour."

"You did. I've just decided we're going to spend the rest of it packing." The check came and he shelled out a few bills to cover it.

Her brown knit in confusion. "Excuse me?"

He slid out of the booth. "Come on, Jennifer. The sooner we get this over, the sooner you can get some sleep."

"Get what over?" She allowed him to pull her from the booth and didn't protest as he led her to the door.

"Packing. I just told you that." He jerked his own coat off the peg and shoved her arms into it. "You're not spending another night in that dump."

The unfamiliar coat distracted her. She looked down at the long sleeves that eclipsed her hands. "This isn't my coat."

"It'll keep you warm. Let's go." He put her slicker over his head and pulled her out the door. It was a sign of how tired she was that she ran behind him without any significant hesitation. He helped her into the Jeep, then skirted the hood and climbed behind the wheel, throwing the slicker onto the backseat.

"What happened to the other car?"

"It's at home." He put the key in the ignition, and the engine roared to life. He backed out of the parking space, then waited for directions before pulling out into the street. "Which way?"

"Where?"

"The dump. Right or left?" He wasn't leaving her with any choice, and he refused to feel guilty about it.

"I told you before, Matt," she said in a perplexed voice. "I don't want you there."

He tried to keep the anger out of his expression. "I'm only going to be there long enough for you to pack and get out. You're coming to my house tonight."

"Your house?"

As in, *the moon*? He would have laughed if he hadn't been so damned sure he was doing the right thing. "My house. I refuse to let you sleep in that dump another night. Now, which way is it?"

"*You* refuse." She gave a disbelieving laugh and pointed to the right. "Where do you get off telling me where I can sleep and where I can't?"

He pulled onto the road and concentrated on trying not to hit anyone in the downpour. "Your self-described dump is so bad you won't even let me see it. I wouldn't be able to live with myself if I let you stay there."

"Again, I have to ask, what business is this of yours?"

He pulled the Jeep to the curb and slammed on the brakes. Keeping his hands on the wheel, he glared at her. "You made it my business when you left your kisses in my dreams."

Her brow furrowed. "That's not what this is about, Matt. Whatever is between us has nothing to do with where I choose to live."

"Wrong." He shook his head vehemently. "I can't feel what I do for you and spend every minute worrying about your safety."

"I managed to take pretty good care of myself in Honolulu."

He scowled. "If this dump is as bad as I imagine, you're going to have to be on guard every minute you're there." He took a couple of deep, even breaths, then caught her gaze with his. "I have two spare rooms. You can have your pick."

"My own room?"

"Your own room." He reached across the space between them to smooth the lines from her brow. "I'm not taking you home just to share my bed. That's beside the point. I want you in a place where you can feel safe and get the rest you need."

"Will you?" Her voice was a thready whisper that coiled around his heart.

He pretended not to understand, just so that she'd know he did think of other things. "Will I what, sweet?"

"Will you ask me to share your bed?"

"Absolutely." His smile was strained because she hadn't agreed yet to come at all. Her safety came first. The rest would happen in its natural time. "If you'll think back, we've already agreed that making love together is a matter of when, not if."

"I remember."

"The anticipation is making it better," he murmured huskily. "Every night I go to bed without you and wonder if the next time I fall asleep, you'll be with me. Tired from lovemaking, your skin tingling because you want to do it again."

Her soft, irregular breaths reached his ears. "I think I'd like that."

"Sharing my bed? Or making love and then doing it again, right away, before either of us has even caught our breath?"

She nodded. "Both."

He drew a ragged breath of his own. Her sensual honesty was going to be the death of him. "Soon, sweet. Very soon. Probably not tonight, though." His hand dropped to the stick shift and flexed around it. "When you come to my bed, I want you to be awake enough to know what's happening. The first time, anyway."

"Are you sure about this, Matt?" she asked softly. "You know you don't have to give me a place to live just to satisfy a few fantasies."

His jaw tightened as he stifled the urge to throttle her. Lord, did she really think he was moving her for his sexual convenience? He tried to make it as clear as he could. "We're going to make love, Jennifer, whether you're living in a dump or in my home. I know it. You know it. I would prefer it wasn't the dump, but it's your choice. I don't like you living in the dump, but I can't force you out of it."

He threw the Jeep into gear and continued down the road. He'd done everything he could, short of tying her up and taking her to his home without her consent. He was trying to decide if he could actually get away with that when she tapped him on the arm.

"You need to turn around, Matt."

"Why?"

"You're going the wrong way." She pointed in the opposite direction. "The dump is about ten blocks back."

Nine

"I'm only staying as long as it takes me to find a cheap, decent place to live," Jennifer said, grabbing the door handle as Matt swung the Jeep around the corner.

He didn't take his eyes off the road. "Whatever you want. The house is big enough for the both of us in the meantime."

He could afford to be generous now that he'd managed to extract her from that dump some slumlord had the audacity to call an apartment. It had been worse than he'd imagined—cheap furniture on cheap linoleum with naked bulbs hanging down from the ceiling and nothing to speak of in the way of heat. Matt had taken one look and known that he would have taken her out of there with or without her permission.

Luckily, she'd been as relieved to put the dump behind her as he'd been to see her go.

She turned to look at him. "It might make more sense if I just try to find a room in someone's house. I would imagine I could find something like that around a university or college, don't you?"

"Don't worry about it tonight, Jennifer. I'll help you look after you've rested up some." He pulled into the driveway and punched the button for the garage door.

"Tomorrow is Sunday, Matt. It's the best day for checking out the rental ads in the paper."

He parked the Jeep beside the Jaguar and shot her a frustrated scowl. "So we'll check them out. Don't you think you can wait until you've had a good night's sleep before you worry about how fast you can get moved?"

"Sorry," she whispered. "It's just that—"

He reached over to cup her chin in one hand. "It's just that you're too tired to think straight. Let's get you to bed before all those plans of yours start spilling out of your head."

He didn't wait for an answer. Sliding out of the Jeep, he opened the backdoor and picked up the single box that held everything she currently possessed. Packing hadn't taken any time, considering all she had were the few things she'd bought, supplemented by what he'd loaned her that belonged to his sister. Nothing had arrived as yet from Pilau or Montana, she'd told him, and she was concerned because the post office might not be able to track her down. They'd deal with the post office on Monday, he'd told her before she could make a case for staying in the dump until her possessions arrived.

Matt hefted the box under one arm and opened the kitchen door, leaving Jennifer to follow. "I'll give you a tour tomorrow, after you've had some rest," he said over his shoulder, heading straight for the stairs.

She hurried to keep up with him. "This is a huge house. What on earth do you need with all this room?"

"It's not as big as it looks." Three bedrooms, three baths, a den, family room, and so on was perhaps more than he needed now, but big enough for a family to grow into.

He stopped at the top of the stairs to switch on a night-light, just in case Jennifer was prone to wandering at night. Passing his own bedroom, he opened the door next to it, praying he'd remembered to straighten it up after his last visitor—whenever that had been. He couldn't recall. His hand found the light switch on the wall. A quick glance reassured him. The bed was made, and it didn't look as if too much dust had accumulated on the dresser.

He put her box down on the only chair in the room. "The bathroom is right across the hall. My bedroom is the next door down."

His gaze followed hers as she checked out the room. Bed, dresser, chair. Not exactly luxurious, but it had all the necessities. Still, he wished he'd taken the time to do more than hang blinds across the windows.

"This is terrific, Matt." She slid a glance at him that was strangely misty. "Thank you for letting me come here. I think I'll sleep better tonight than I have in weeks." She shrugged out of his coat and handed it to him.

"Then I'll let you get to it." He backed out into the hallway, his hands fisted in the folds of the coat. "I'll be up for a while yet, if you need anything. Good night."

Ignoring her startled gaze, he turned on his heel and headed back downstairs. Without turning on the lights, he strode into the living room and flung himself into the papa-san chair. The rain had reduced to a drizzle, though it still obscured the stars and moon and the reflected lights of other homes on the lake. He sat in the dark and stared into a night that was pitch-black and endless.

He could hear Jennifer moving around upstairs, that soft click of either the bedroom or bathroom door as she prepared to settle down for the night. He hoped she wouldn't need anything, that she wouldn't come down those stairs, because he just might not be as in control of himself later as he was now. He might take her in his arms, as he'd wanted to do from the moment they'd pulled into the garage. He might just start kissing her . . . and never stop until he was buried deep inside her with her legs wrapped around his hips and her arms holding him as though she'd never let go.

No, not tonight. He'd already promised her that,

more or less. Hell, he might even wait until she'd found a place of her own before he let the sexual part of their relationship resume. Or begin. Whatever.

How could he make love to her in this house and not be teased by the memories every time he walked in the door?

Then again, would it really matter where he loved her? Would he ever be able to forget Jennifer?

Matt let out a long, slow breath and sank deeper into the cushions. The sensible thing now would be to help her find that apartment and get her out of his house. They would date and have whatever level of relationship she would allow. Then they would say good-bye when the time came for her to leave. Jennifer would go off on her world tour and he would get on with the rest of his life in the best way he could.

He wanted more. He wanted her there, with him, more than he wanted his next breath.

Even if it was only for a few months, he wanted to share his life with her in every way there was. It would be their only chance.

Propping his feet on the horsehair footstool, Matt closed his eyes and wondered if she was asleep yet. Or would she spend the night worrying about the thousand and one things that someone who was homeless, jobless, and essentially stranded worried about?

He wished he could at least convince her to stay a little longer, save her precious resources as she looked for a job. It would make so much sense to wait until she knew where she'd be working before she committed to any kind of a lease or rental agreement.

He couldn't bear the thought of her leaving.

It had been a long day. Matt yawned and rubbed his eyes, and thought he should get upstairs before he fell asleep where he was. It was so comfortable, though. And besides, Jennifer was upstairs.

Maybe he'd wait until he could be certain she was asleep. Another yawn overtook him, and his head dug into the cushions of the chair. He'd move later, when she was asleep. He'd go up to bed then.

• • •

Matt's feet fell from the footstool with a resounding crash.

"Damn!" Matt sat up, rubbing the kink from his neck as he cursed himself for falling asleep in the chair when there was a perfectly good bed upstairs. Three of them, actually, but one was already taken.

By Jennifer. Too bad he couldn't convince her to stay, make her realize that she wasn't taking anything from him by sleeping in a bed that was rarely used. But Jennifer wouldn't take when she couldn't give, and there wasn't anything he could do about that.

He could let her give!

Matt sucked in a quick breath, then let it out slowly as the idea took shape in his mind. He'd been going about this all wrong. Demanding that Jennifer take his help had only succeeded because she'd been desperate to leave that apartment anyhow. But she wouldn't stay long, not unless he could give her a reason. A job. Sort of.

She could help him take care of his house in exchange for a place to live. There was always something that needed doing, and heaven knew he didn't always get around to even the most basic chores.

What if she hated housework?

Then maybe she could do something else, like pull weeds or wash the car. She could even cook if she wanted to. It would be a treat to eat something that hadn't been grilled outside—his only cooking skill and a tad inconvenient when it rained.

Having someone in the house when he was gone would be a plus. What with the newspapers that he almost always forgot to suspend, the mail, and whatever else landed on his doorstep, the house was a prime target for thieves.

Jennifer could make his home safe. He thought she'd get a kick out of that.

His excitement drove him to his feet, and he paced in front of the windows as he considered the arguments he would face when he made his proposition. He checked his watch and muttered an oath because it was only two o'clock.

Perhaps she was an early riser. He hoped so, since he certainly wouldn't be getting any more rest until this was settled.

"I heard a noise."

He halted his pacing at the sound of her voice. He wouldn't have to wait until morning. Turning, he saw her hesitating at the end of the room, clothed in a long, sleeveless nightgown that hinted at her feminine curves and fell to a gentle swirl above her bare feet. The light from the kitchen gave her silhouette an ethereal look, a delicacy that was at odds with the strong, determined woman he'd come to know.

"The footstool took a header," he said. "Nothing to worry about." He held out his hand. "I need to talk to you. Come."

She smiled shyly and shook her head. "I'm not dressed."

"I noticed." He smiled back, not forcing the issue because it was for the best if she stayed over there. Holding her close, he might forget the arguments he'd created to negate her protests.

It was important he get this right.

He shoved is hands into his back pockets and outlined the basics without allowing her to interrupt. Her expression changed as he spoke, beginning with doubtful, toying with wary, and finally ending with a glimmer of hope he could see even though they were so far apart.

He gave her a minute, then couldn't stand the suspense any longer. "So what do you think, Jennifer? You said it was a big house. I could certainly use some help with it."

"I would have thought you'd already have someone coming in to clean." She rubbed her palms against her sides in a nervous gesture. "I couldn't consider it if I'm putting someone else out of a job. I certainly know how that feels."

"There's no one else to worry about. I'm here so

irregularly, it's hard to get someone to come in on any kind of schedule. I manage on my own for the most part, although you have to admit I don't do the best job you've ever seen." He hoped she'd noticed the dust on the dresser upstairs.

"You do okay." She regarded him curiously. "How did you know that I like housework?"

"I don't . . . I didn't." He stumbled across the words as a tendril of hope inched into his heart. "I guess I just hoped."

"My mom said I was a throwback to another age." She smiled crookedly. "I *like* cooking and cleaning and making a house feel like a home." Her gaze narrowed on the shadows of the assorted furnishings, and she frowned. "I'm not sure I've seen anything quite like this before."

"Just a few things I've picked up on my travels," he said proudly. "Wait until daylight and I'll give you a grand tour of my treasures."

Her face took on a look of disbelief that he didn't understand. "I'm sure everything will look lovely in the morning," she said enigmatically.

He leaned down to right the footstool, then walked around to stand behind the papa-san chair. His fingers curled around the rattan frame of its fanned back. "You're sure about this Jennifer? Cleaning and cooking aren't the most glamorous pastimes I can think of."

"I'm sure." She glanced away as if nervous. "About the cooking—"

He interrupted before she could talk herself out of it. "I don't expect gourmet meals, sweet. The basics will do nicely."

A smile flitted across her face, and she shrugged. "I should be able to manage the basics."

"You'll scrub toilets too?" he teased.

"We'll flip for that one."

"Deal." He allowed himself to relax. Jennifer was going to stay. Here, where she belonged. "I think I'm going to like knowing that you'll be here when I come home."

"It's only for a few months, until I get a nanny job," she reminded him softly. "Don't get too used to it."

"Don't talk about leaving," he said roughly.

"Moving in with you won't affect my plans. You've got to understand that, Matt."

He swallowed hard. "I understand, sweet. I just don't want to talk about it."

"All right." She cocked her head and regarded him thoughtfully. "There is one thing you need to know."

"What's that?"

"If I'd gone back to Pilau like I was supposed to, part of me would have always wondered what it would be like to be with you; to lie in your arms and learn what excites you." The tip of her tongue slid between her lips, leaving them wet and glistening. "I'm not sorry things turned out like they did."

His heart lurched, then thudded against his chest. "You're so honest about your feelings, it sometimes scares me."

"You don't like it?"

"I like it too much maybe." He took a deep breath, fighting for control. It was a losing battle, though, and not one he really wanted to win anyway. "I find it incredibly erotic that you say exactly what you feel."

"I haven't had much practice at making love. And at this point in my life, I don't have the luxury of worrying about saying the right things."

"You haven't said anything wrong yet," he murmured. "I think you say what you feel because you like hearing it too." His gaze drifted down from her face to where her small, firm breasts pushed against the fabric of her gown. "Do you remember in Hawaii when I said something about kissing you behind the closed door of my room?"

Her hands curled into fists at her sides. She gave a nearly imperceptible nod but didn't speak. Perhaps, he thought, her throat was as dry as his.

"I knew then," he went on, "that you liked images. I'm glad we'll have a chance to explore that affinity we both seem to share."

He moved toward her very slowly. "I would have come to Pilau, sweet. I haven't told you that before, have I?" He was close enough to smell her special scent of flowers and spring. "Maybe not right away, but it wouldn't have been long. Those fantasies were driving me out of my mind."

He reached out a hand to stroke the soft hairs that curled in front of her ear. "One of them started like this, with me still dressed and you in your night-gown. We were in the bedroom, though. Standing at the foot of my bed. Only you weren't facing me." His touch was light but firm on her shoulders as he turned her around. "I was behind you, touching you without letting you touch me. It drove you a little wild, I think. I know it excited me."

He heard her soft gasp and smiled. "Go upstairs, Jennifer. You know which room is mine. I'll be up as soon as I turn out the lights."

He had to get her started. With a hand between her shoulder blades, he gently pushed her toward the stairs. She gave him a last look over her shoulder, her expression filled with a nervous excitement that he recognized because it was exactly how he felt. Nervous and excited.

And more aroused than he would have thought possible.

Matt took his time closing up the house. He checked the doors and the windows, and finally turned out the lights before walking up the stairs. She would be waiting for him, he knew. Wondering why it was taking so long . . . thinking about what they were going to do.

Anticipation was an ingredient to lovemaking he'd never enjoyed so much as he did at that moment. He hoped she appreciated it too.

Reaching the top of the staircase, he paused at the night-light. He would leave it on, he decided. It would provide all the light they needed for now.

It was just enough for him to see where Jennifer stood waiting, her white gown picking up the meager light and drawing his gaze. She was at the bottom of the bed, as he'd described, her back to him and her arms at her sides. Moving quietly, he walked up behind her and lifted her hair from her nape. His mouth touched her there, ever so softly, and he felt the tremor that shook her as he trailed a wet kiss across her sensitive skin.

"I think the most exciting part of this fantasy is the beginning," he murmured, finding her hips with his hands and urging her to lean against him. "I touch, you feel. I'm dressed, you're naked." He gave a low laugh and caught the cotton gown between his fingers. "Well, almost naked. It won't be long, though, sweet. I want you to enjoy the textures for a bit before I take the gown away."

"Do I get to take part in this?" she asked, a slightly miffed note in her voice as she squirmed against him.

It was all he could do not to take her then and there, without preliminaries, without even trying to give her the kind of pleasure she deserved. Matt took a deep breath, then nuzzled her shoulder. "Eventually. But not too soon, if you don't mind. I've been wanting you for so long that if you touch me, I'm likely to go up in flames—with or without you."

"How do you think I feel now?"

He laughed and again took that as an invitation. "I don't know, Jennifer. Why don't we see exactly how you feel. I have to admit I've been wondering. . . ."

His fingers spread across her belly, kneading, petting, letting her feel his heat through her gown. Her head fell back into the curve of his shoulder as he ventured downward, learning her curves through the barrier of cotton, until his fingers discovered the springy cushion of hair between her legs.

Her soft cry spurred him to a greater urgency, and though he knew he should take this slowly, he couldn't seem to remember the reason for it.

He wanted to be inside her more than he wanted to breathe.

Matt wedged his hands between her legs and pushed outward, having no words for what he wanted. She wanted it, too, because she parted her legs and grasped his upper arms for support.

He didn't hesitate. His fingers probed her feminine secrets, caressing her through the gown that wasn't a barrier at all. The cotton became damp with her arousal, her heat clinging to his fingers and making him want more.

He quickly dispensed with the gown, gathering it in his hands and tucking it beneath her arms. Above her breasts. He made sure she kept it there, giving her silent signals that she read as if she'd known the language forever. Her hands were clenched around his biceps, her nails digging soft moons into his skin. He murmured sweet words of encouragement followed by hot, exciting words of passion. Could she feel how hard he was beneath his jeans? he asked. Did she like how the denim rubbed against her fanny?

Did she know that if she touched him now, he'd be inside her before she could draw her next breath?

He cupped her small breasts in his hands, kneading them, delighting in her hard nipples. Were her nipples sensitive to a light touch or a heavy one? he asked, then experimented for himself when she wasn't quick enough with a response.

Both, he discovered. He couldn't wait, he told her, to see how she liked his mouth suckling, nibbling. She sagged against him, a telling clue that the fantasy was too much for their first time together.

Too much, too long. He needed to be inside her. He should have known better than to pick tonight for this particular fantasy. It required an endurance he didn't have at the moment.

His hands flew back to the source of her heat. He opened the swollen flower of her sex with care, his fingers sliding against her as he sought to pleasure her, his thumb beginning an insistent massage against the hard nud at its center. She cried out, her words indistinguishable, but he knew what she was saying because he wanted the same thing.

Still he hesitated.

He put one arm around her waist for support and slid a single finger into the moist passage. She was so hot and tight he worried for a moment he might hurt her. He tested her with a second finger, and discovered a resiliency that both reassured him and drove him mad.

He needed her. Now, without any more preliminaries. And she was more than ready. Her quivering response clutched at his fingers as he slowly withdrew.

"Raise your arms, sweet." She did, and he pulled the gown from her body and threw it aside. He slid his arm under her legs and lifted her against him. She slipped her arms around his neck and pulled his mouth down to hers.

He kissed her just once, a hard, almost impatient exchange that was over almost before it had begun. Moving quickly to the head of the bed, he pulled back the quilt and blanket and laid her on the cool sheets. He threw off his clothes, fumbled with the foil packet of protection he pulled out of the bedside drawer, then found his place between her legs.

He laced his fingers with hers, took the weight of his body on his elbows, and angled himself to enter her. She made it easy, lifting her hips, sliding a single leg around his waist as he nudged the opening to her silken sheath. He entered her in a long, explosive thrust that he'd remember as long as he lived.

He was lost. His hands tightened around hers as he lay without moving, his heart barely remembering the rhythm of life. He took one deep breath, then another. He'd never been this out of control, this vulnerable, and he couldn't imagine that he was impressing Jennifer.

The muscles in his butt clenched as he tried to remember this was a lady beneath him, a woman who deserved her own pleasure before or while he took his.

God, he hoped she was ready. The hesitation was costing him his mind.

"I can't wait any longer, sweet," he finally said, his hips beginning to move before the words were out. "I'm sorry it's so fast. . . ."

"It's about time, Matt. I was wondering if you'd lost interest."

"I'm trying to be considerate, dammit. You're so small." He groaned because the ecstasy of being inside her was so close to pain. "I don't want to hurt you."

"I'm not hurt."

He found her gaze in the darkness that surrounded them. "And I don't want to leave you behind. Notice that I'm trying very hard to do this right our first time."

"I noticed." She lifted her head and kissed his cheek. "I think you don't need to worry about me."

He kissed her back. "Sure?"

"Sure." Her laugh found a nerve at the base of his spine. "Think you can keep up?"

What? His mind kicked out of gear as she moved beneath him. She lifted him, her hips thrusting and releasing, her arms tightening around his back, dragging him down to her. He gave in to the explosive pace she set, to the need to feel her body against his. Her breasts were crushed beneath him, her hard nipples playing their own game of torture across his chest.

His mouth found hers as the pressure built in his loins. He swallowed her cries, his tongue mating with hers, then letting go as the pace she set made it impossible to hold the kiss. He pushed his face into the pillow beside her head, holding her hands still, because it seemed it was the only thing he had left to hang on to.

He felt her shudder beneath him, then again as muscles that held him intimately began to convulse. It was time.

She hadn't waited for him after all.

With a shout of elation, he followed her into the mist of rapture and found her waiting for him there.

Smiling her joy.

Ten

It was early morning when Matt awakened to find Jennifer curled into a ball beside him, her tush wedged in the cradle of his hips, her back warm against his chest, her head nestled beneath the curve of his arm. His other arm lay atop her, his hand spread across her smooth, satiny thigh.

At least, he guessed that was where all the body parts were positioned. She was invisible beneath the covers, with even her head hidden from sight. Only a few wisps of silky hair escaped her cocoon to adorn the pillow beside his face.

It was a miracle that she could even breathe under there, he thought. He pulled the quilt downward, tucking it beneath her chin. Her lashes fluttered against her cheeks, and as he watched, a sweet, dreamy smile touched her lips. When her nose twitched and a small fist broke cover to rub it, he was convinced she was in the early states of waking up.

That was fine with Matt. The ache in his groin that had been the cause of his own awakening was growing worse.

She sighed and snuggled closer, her sleep-warmed skin an erotic rub against his. His gaze narrowed on her face to discover her eyes were still closed. Firmly. So much for waking up.

He would have to help her along.

His hand slid along the flare of her hip, his thumb stroking the soft hollow that verged on her flat stomach. She was particularly sensitive there, but then, Jennifer was sensitive in a lot of places.

His thumb trailed over the silken skin, back and forth, gradually increasing the span of the caress until he'd reached the nest of curls between her legs. She moved against him in her sleep, her back arching away from his chest when his fingers threaded with insistent precision into the springy curls. Almost in slow motion, her legs uncurled, her feet inching down his legs until the backs of her thighs were warm against his.

His hand retreated to her belly, where his widespread fingers began an emphatic massage. Raising up on an elbow, he watched her face carefully. He wanted to know the exact moment she awakened because that was when he would take her. When she opened her eyes to meet his, he would thrust into her tight, hot sheath and confirm what he'd come to accept in the early hours before dawn.

They belonged together.

Twice that night, they'd made love. Each time, he'd felt as if he were losing a part of himself as he explored dimensions of pleasure he'd never before envisioned. Jennifer took that part of him that slipped from his soul and gave him such joy in return that he didn't even miss it.

The act of making love had never been so intimate as it was with Jennifer. So perfect.

He didn't know how he would cope when she was gone.

Matt shoved aside that disturbing thought as he concentrated on the woman in his arms. Lord, but she was a heavy sleeper, he mused. His palm grazed her nipples, yet still her eyes remained closed. Her face snuggled deeper into the crook of his arm, and he would have quit his teasing were it not for one thing.

Even in her sleep, she responded to him.

His breath caught in his throat as he felt her

nipples push erect and rigid at his caress. There was no going back.

Reaching across her to the bedside table, he groped in the drawer and pulled out a foil packet. He had to move away from her to take care of her protection, an absence she noticed. She whimpered and shifted until she was against him again. He finished what he was doing with a frustrated jerk, threw off the too-warm covers, then put his arms around her again, bringing her fanny tight against his arousal.

Home.

He groaned aloud at the exquisite pressure. Sweet heaven, she excited him like no other woman. He put his mouth on her neck as his hand fluttered down her belly to her thighs. She gave a tiny moan and said something unintelligible under her breath. His gaze followed the path of his hand as he edged it between her thighs and raised her upper leg, then he tucked his knee into the gap between her legs.

When his hand curved back around her hip and across her belly, she was open for him. Open and moist. He curled his hand around the intimate center of her and pressed. She moaned again and pushed back. He inserted two fingers into the slick canal of her heat, testing the strength of her response. She tightened around him and pressed her own hand on top of his.

He bent his head and sucked her earlobe between his teeth.

Her eyes flew open.

"At last," he growled, and took her mouth in a deep, hungry kiss as he rolled her onto her back. He pulled her thighs high around his waist and sank into her, lifting her higher, closer, tighter . . . until she'd taken all of him.

The rhythm of their bodies eclipsed all that was real and sane. He rocked with her, against her, answering the thrust of her hips with a force that should have driven her right through the bed, but didn't. Her tongue mated with his as she gave up the most precious cries of pleasure he'd ever heard. Her legs tightened against him as her arms curled around his shoulders with a force that threatened never to ease.

He supported her with one arm around her hips as his other hand found and stroked her just millimeters above where they were joined.

Suddenly, she tensed in his arms. He held himself still, reveling in the magic of it all as she stood poised on the brink of her release.

"Now, sweet?" he murmured, even though he already knew her well enough not to have to ask. She was ready—waiting for him, trying to hold back so that they could crest the wave together. She glared up at him with eyes that were feverish with her desire.

Oh, yes, she was ready. He just wanted to hear her say it.

"Now," she panted, perspiration beading on her forehead as her head tossed on the pillow, her hair a flaming tangle beneath her. "If you wouldn't mind, Colonel . . ."

He didn't. He withdrew until only the very tip of him was inside her. Holding her wild gaze with his, he slid back in, taking his time, relishing the exquisite sensation as she tried to recapture him, keep him. He grinned, and did it again. And again. The pace quickened, partly because she insisted, but more because he couldn't stand it anymore.

She found her release first, tears sliding down her cheeks as she cried out and shuddered uncontrollably beneath him. Then she laughed and tightened her hold around him, giving him urging he didn't need but wouldn't have denied for the world.

Finally, when he thought he'd explode, he did. Into a thousand fragments, a blinding light bursting in his head, bells and firecrackers ringing in his ears. Matt felt another piece of his soul escape, and he gave a hoarse shout as Jennifer replaced the void with something uniquely hers.

The spirit of her joy filled him and made him whole.

She was gone. Matt's hand groped the sheets next to him and came up empty.

Where the hell was she?

He sat straight up in bed. A vague clanging noise reached his ears. She was in the house. Not in this room, but here, nevertheless. The kitchen, he guessed.

She hadn't gone after all.

He breathed a giant sigh of relief and fell back against the pillows. It made no sense, of course, that she would leave.

Not after the night they'd spent together.

He winced at his arrogance and tried to put things into perspective. She was still here because . . .

Because she needed a place to live, and he'd provided her with the opportunity to stay there without seeming to take . . . to take charity. She would work her fanny off to earn her keep. Not exactly what he'd intended, but there wasn't much he could do to tone down her independence.

Perhaps she was still there because she had wanted what had passed between them last night as much as he. Yes, she'd been enthusiastic and giving.

Yes, she'd been warm.

She'd been loving.

More than he could have hoped.

It was going to be a problem letting her go. And if he ever managed that, how could he possibly continue to live in this house and not be constantly reminded of the woman with whom he'd fallen in love but couldn't have?

Matt stared blindly across the room, considering his options, limited as they were. And the consequences.

He loved her, had probably even begun his short but entirely thorough fall for Jennifer on the tarmac at Pilau. From the beginning, she'd worked her way into his heart.

She would be there until he drew his last breath.

It explained so much, and complicated everything. The fantasies, the dreams . . . they were unlike anything he'd ever experienced. Tenuous, unyielding, and insistent, her soul had become a part of him in such a way that he knew he would never be whole again without her.

The reality of loving her filled his heart close to bursting.

He needed to resign himself to living without her, though. He didn't have another choice. Jennifer had plans he didn't dare try to alter, a life that was full of travel to places he'd already seen. He couldn't take that away from her, the adventures that were still to come. He couldn't take those, not without stealing an essential part of her spirit.

He loved her, but she wasn't to know that. Her dream had to come first.

The clatter of pots and pans from the kitchen roused him from his thoughts. It was time to confront his dilemma.

How could he get through the day and not tell her the truth? He was worrying through Plan A and Plan B when the phone rang.

It was Uncle Ricky, ha-ha, calling to see if he wanted to bat the ball around on the base courts and perhaps put together a real set of tennis . . . or was the old man too weary after his last trip. Germany had been a skate, Rick had heard, though the brief stop in England didn't sound like much of a picnic, what with one engine out and a blown tire in the same go.

Matt shrugged off the mission's complications with a snort. What's the job about if it isn't challenges? he asked.

Rick laughed and said that was why Matt was a lieutenant colonel and he was still a captain. Challenges of that sort he'd rather see later than sooner.

So was he up for a match or two?

Matt told Uncle Ricky exactly what he'd do to him on the courts, given time, then turned down the match. He wasn't going to be in town long enough.

"I'm on my way out," he said, throwing off the covers and heading toward the closet. "Maybe when I get back."

"But you just landed yesterday," Rick said. "Five days out equals at least two days crew rest."

"Not this time." Matt said good-bye and replaced the receiver. Rick knew the regulations as well as he, and was well aware that unless they were at war or worse, there was no power in the air force that could drag him back to work before tomorrow evening at the earliest.

Matt pulled a clean flight suit from the closet, then went into the bathroom for a quick shower. Just ten minutes later, he was shaved and dressed. As he hadn't bothered to unpack the night before, it was a simple matter of replacing dirty clothes with clean and zipping the bag. He was ready to leave before he was ready . . .

He couldn't stay and face her, talk to her. Not yet.

He needed to learn how to let her go. Then, perhaps, he could be rational about this.

In the meantime, the house was hers. She would be safe here.

He grabbed the green B4 bag and trotted down the stairs. He found her in the kitchen, her jeans-clad butt sticking out from beneath a lower cabinet.

It was so damned difficult to look at that sweet, curvy tush and not want to strip down to nothing and join her.

He couldn't, though. He was on a mission.

That's what they called it in the air force. A mission.

Another word for escape.

"Jennifer."

He winced as her head connected with the cabinet.

She rubbed the top of her head as she backed out of the cabinet. "You could have stamped your feet or something before scaring me half to death."

He gave a half grin. "I'd ask what you were doing in there, but I bet I wouldn't understand."

She sat up on her knees and gave him a look that was probably meant to reprimand. "I can't believe you've lived here a year and haven't even bothered with shelf paper."

He stared at her, her hair tumbling loose from a high ponytail, her face streaked with something he didn't want to know about, her eyes glistening with mischief. How could he ever walk into this house again and not think of her? "Shelf paper?" he asked, a smile tugging at one corner of his mouth. "What's that?"

She ignored him, her gaze narrowing on his flight suit. "Why are you wearing that?"

He took a deep breath and lied. "The phone call. I have to leave."

"Now?" She looked as though the wind had been knocked out of her.

He nodded. "Now."

She lowered her gaze and rose to her feet, moving to the counter that separated them. "I would have thought you got more time off between trips than a single day."

He shrugged. "I go when I'm told," he said, counting on the fact that she was ignorant enough about the system not to argue. "In the meantime, this will give you a chance to settle in." He reached into the drawer beneath the telephone and pulled out an extra set of keys. "These are for the house. Be sure you lock all the doors when you leave. And at night."

"I'm not stupid," she muttered.

"And these other two are for the Jeep. I'm assuming you can manage a four-wheel-drive."

Her lashes fluttered, then lifted to reveal her reluctant gaze. "I can, but I wasn't aware a vehicle came with the deal."

He pressed the keys into her palm. "We're living on a lake at the end of nowhere, Jennifer. Public transport will get you around if you've got the time and patience. The Jeep will save on both counts."

"I buy gas." She gave him the same look she'd used on Load in Pilau. Matt found it difficult to hide his smile.

"You buy gas," he agreed.

She said quickly, "How long will you be gone?"

He shook his head, and cupped her chin in his hand . . . a chin that he could have sworn was strangely tense. "I don't know, sweet. I'll call if I can."

"Where are you going?" she whispered, her eyes filling with an emotion he didn't want to see.

"Can't say." That implied top secret, although he really meant he didn't have a clue. He'd find out after he squeezed a trip out of the schedulers. He took a deep breath and planted a quick, hard kiss on her lips.

Lips that were trembling.

Lips that were sweeter than any he'd tasted before.

Lips that he couldn't imagine not kissing every day and night for the rest of his life.

"Save the receipts for whatever you spend on the house," he said. "Shelf paper and whatever else. Do you have enough cash to get by?"

She nodded. "I'll manage."

His gaze narrowed at her. "Enough for food?"

A rebellious expression filled her eyes. "Food *and* gas. Go on your trip, Colonel. I'll do just fine here."

He sighed over her anger. "I know you will, sweet. Probably better than either of us can imagine." He gave her another quick kiss, then turned away.

He had to leave now . . . or never.

He let himself out through the garage door and threw his bag into the Jag, then returned to the laundry room to collect the other bags that contained all his in-flight, things-that-pilots-need-to-have gear.

She wasn't in the kitchen when he passed through that last time.

Perhaps she felt as he did, that long good-byes were harder than short ones.

He backed the small car into the street with a

growl from both man and machine, then headed for McChord.

He would go to the squadron and demand to be on the first trip he was eligible for. At least twenty-four hours from now, though, because he'd just returned and they weren't operating in wartime conditions.

He would get a room on base in the bachelor officer quarters—BOQs.

He would stay away from Jennifer and figure out how he'd ever get used to being with her while he knew that, someday, he'd have to let her go.

Eleven

The late-afternoon sun slanted through a low-hanging mist, the glare all but blinding Matt as he tooled down the interstate toward home. Home and Jennifer. He was going back where he belonged, before he could change his mind. Again.

He'd really intended to stay away from her for more than a handful of hours. Fortunately, his intentions were overcome by something much stronger.

Common sense.

If he was going to deal with Jennifer, it wouldn't be by running away. He should have known better than to try.

He hoped she wouldn't ask too many questions about his early return. He felt enough of a fool already, what with the scene he'd caused at the squadron. He had all but fallen to his knees and begged for a slot on a trip. Any trip, as long as it left as soon as he was legal to fly again. Any slot, even if it meant riding in the third seat and getting no stick time at all.

They'd given him the two-day turn to Tinker Air Force Base in Oklahoma the following evening, a run that normally fell to much less senior fliers. Pilots of Matt's rank usually managed to avoid those less exciting trips. The schedulers had waffled about replacing either of the slated pilots, but, in the end, had given in and let Matt have the number-two job—copilot. Number one, the aircraft commander, fell to a young captain who had a quarter of Matt's experience and was still in awe—or pretended to be—of any rank higher than his own.

It would be a long trip.

Ignoring the snickering that had followed him out of the scheduling office, he'd gone over to the BOQs to book a room. Without official orders, which would have precluded the need to pay, he'd had to fork over eight dollars for the privilege of staying in a place that wasn't home . . . but close enough to it that he could make the drive in thirty minutes.

He'd checked out two hours later without bothering to ask for his money back. The important thing was to get back to Jennifer, he'd realized after nearly pacing a trench down the center of the room. He needed to deal with his feelings without running away from them.

She didn't have to know what was going on in his head. The facts of the situation weren't going to change, no matter how long and hard he stared at them.

He loved Jennifer.

He couldn't tell her.

She would leave him one day soon.

So be it.

It was time to quit whining like a three-year-old and enjoy whatever time he had with her. Matt swung the car off the interstate and took the shortest route to his house. It was harder on the shocks, thanks to a series of speed bumps in the parking lot he detoured across, but well worth the thirty seconds he saved by not having to stop at the corner light.

He punched the automatic door opener as he pulled into the driveway. The Jeep was right where he'd left it.

Good. She was home.

Somewhere. He stood in the strangely quiet house and wondered just where she'd gotten to. A quick glance behind the counter revealed a sparkling kitchen floor but little in the way of feminine presence. Matt searched through the ground-floor rooms without success. Upstairs yielded the same results. A frown creased his brow as he strode over to the living-room windows to check outside.

He found her there—not outside, but nearly hidden in the giant cushion of the papa-san chair. She was curled up like a puppy, sleeping as soundly as the proverbial rock. Not a log, he mused, shaking his head, but a rock.

He'd never met anyone who slept as hard as Jennifer.

A wave of silky red curls fell over her eyes. He reached out a hand to push it back, but stopped himself, thinking that if she was that tired, he shouldn't wake her. Getting her to catch up on her rest had been half the point of bringing her there, he reminded himself.

He wanted her to know he was home, but there wasn't any hurry about that. Not really.

Sighing, he pulled back his hand. But as he retreated from the room, he chuckled at his caution. It would take more than a light caress to rouse Jennifer. Still laughing, he climbed the stairs to his bedroom and changed into jeans and an old sweatshirt. It was time he tackled those weeds in the backyard.

After all, he didn't want Jennifer to think he was a complete slob. A little dust was one thing, but neglecting the yard was altogether different. Grabbing a Seattle Mariners baseball cap from the collection at the top of his closet, Matt skipped back down the stairs and let himself out the kitchen door into the garage.

Now, where had he left the wheelbarrow? It had been so long. . . .

Matt checked on Jennifer through the window and shook his head in amazement. Three hours he'd been working outside, and she hadn't moved. As he'd worked through the cool afternoon, thoughts of Jennifer had alternately aroused and diverted him until, at times, it had been nearly impossible to bend over. Still, he'd let her sleep.

She couldn't sleep forever, though. He hoped. It appeared that she needed the rest more than he'd originally imagined. He tugged the baseball cap farther down on his forehead and turned from the windows with a grimace, leaving sleeping beauty to her dreams.

It was probably for the best. After wrestling with the weeds and winning at least part of that battle, he'd gone to work on the hot tub. The chemicals required to keep the water clear and clean came in five-gallon plastic tubs that were guaranteed to spill at the slightest provocation. As a result, he was sweaty and smelled like a rare blend of chlorine and weed killer. Jennifer would likely drop in a dead faint at the first whiff.

The way she slept, he'd hate to think how long it would take for her to recover from a swoon. The image made him grin as he knelt beside the hot tub. He'd just test the chemical levels before taking a quick shower. After all this work, he wasn't about to pollute the hot tub by giving into his druthers and jumping in, not without removing at least the first layer of dirt from his body.

With the plastic vial in one hand, he balanced himself with the other and leaned over the tub to dip—

"Ki-yah!" The bloodcurdling scream cracked through the air a split second before something hard thudded against his butt. Matt was given no time to reflect on the source of the attack as he was driven headfirst into the hot tub, his own roar of outrage cut short as his mouth filled with water.

His forehead connected with the Plexiglas bottom. *Lord, that hurt!* He forced the pain aside and focused on survival. The mouthful of water made its way into his lungs as he frantically tried to orient himself. Up was the opposite of down, he discovered after another disgusting swallow of chlorine. But there was someone up there waiting for him. Was it worth it finding out who . . . or what?

His muddled thinking was quickly replaced by the need to breathe. Planting his feet on the bottom, he silently swore as he realized—irrelevant, but true— that the clean water was now in need of a good cleaning again.

He surged upward, breaking out into the cool evening air with a roar that would have done justice to a B-movie monster. It was hard to mount an offensive without a proper breath, though. He was reduced to wiping his eyes as he coughed up the foul-tasting water. Standing in chest-deep water, he marshaled his defenses and prayed his attacker had taken the opportunity to abscond with the stereo or whatever because he was in no shape to fight back.

Finally, when the fit of coughing subsided and his lungs were again filling with air, he swiped a final trickle of water from his eyes and squinted through the chlorine mist. A slight, slender figure in a yellow sweatsuit and sneakers peered back at him.

"Matt? Are you okay?"

So she was awake. The commotion must have done the trick, he realized, thanking the fates that she hadn't been outside during the attack. It was one thing to have a black belt in karate and quite another to have to use it in her own backyard.

He nodded, and gave another harsh cough. "Did you see the guy? He must have run right past the windows." Matt made a quick visual search of the backyard before returning his gaze to Jennifer. "You didn't try to stop him, did you?"

She was looking so guilty, he knew the answer before she gave it.

"Well, not exactly." She cleared her throat and avoided his gaze.

Of course, she'd tried to stop the attacker. And, apparently, she'd failed. Matt sighed with relief and wondered if he'd ever get used to Jennifer's reckless streak.

He would have been more pleased had she slept through the entire incident. He hated thinking someone was there when she was asleep and so incredibly vulnerable.

He shivered, and it wasn't because of the cold. After crawling out of the hot tub, he shook himself off as best he could and smiled reassuringly at her. "Don't be upset, sweet. It's just as well he got away. I'm sure you scared him enough that we won't have to worry about him coming back."

Jennifer looked down at her feet and groaned. Shivering in earnest now, Matt grabbed her hand and led her into the garage, winding through the chilly gloom until they reached the kitchen door. His sneakers squelched on the parquet floor—something else that would need yet another cleaning—as he crossed to the laundry room and began to shed his clothes.

"Now I'm going to have to do it all over again," he muttered. "Damn, but I wish the guy had tossed me in there *before* I got the hot tub cleaned!"

Jennifer backed against the counter. "Um, Matt—"

"It will have to wait for another day, though," he continued, thinking she just needed a few minutes of normal conversation to regain her equilibrium. She looked as white as a ghost. "I need a good, hot dinner after that dunking. I wonder if there are any steaks in the freezer." Naked, he grabbed a towel from the hamper and ran it over his body.

"You know, Matt, I think there's something—"

He threw the towel on top of the pile of dripping clothes and put his arms around her shoulders. "Come upstairs and tell me," he said, pulling her along with him. "I'm in desperate need of a shower. I can still smell the weed killer through the chlorine."

He wondered if his nudity embarrassed her, because she was flushing now. Perhaps he shouldn't have stripped down in front of her, he mused. Jennifer was such a delicate, innocent little thing. It was hard to tell what was going to bother her.

He would have thought his nudity would be the

last thing on her mind at the moment. But then, he *had* wanted to dispel her fears or whatever she'd been upset about after the attack on him. Perhaps he'd known subconsciously that letting her see him naked would divert her thoughts.

It had been so dark in the bedroom last night. . . .

A flicker of memory made him glance down. The arousal he'd nurtured and fought since arriving home had clearly fallen victim to the violent chain of events. He supposed he should be grateful for small—he chuckled—favors. If she was embarrassed by him in stasis, so to speak, he couldn't imagine what the sight of him fully aroused would do to her.

Getting booted into the hot tub was certainly a novel way of controlling his sexual urges, he mused, then took his thoughts elsewhere before the sweetly intimate ache was resurrected.

He grinned and returned his attention to Jennifer. Intentional or not, his strategy had worked. Her face was even more flushed than before. Taking pity, he pushed her to sit on the edge of the bed, then went into the bathroom. "I won't be a second, sweet. Then we'll sit down over a glass of wine—or soda—and you can tell me what the guy looked like. I didn't even get a glimpse of him."

"But, Matt—"

"I'll hurry, Jennifer. Why don't you pull something out of the closet for me to wear." He ducked out of sight and wondered if she would be there when he came out of the shower. Perhaps he should wear a towel when he went back into the bedroom.

Strange, though. After the way she'd spoken of wanting to make love with him, the way she'd fallen in with the fantasy last night . . . Matt shook his head in confusion. No, he wouldn't have thought nudity would embarrass her.

Reaching into the shower, he turned the water to just short of boiling and took a hard look at himself in the mirror. Cautiously, he lifted his fingers to his forehead and explored the bump he found there. The skin wasn't broken, but he'd have a goose egg before much longer.

He wondered what the flight surgeon would have to say about it. Nothing, he decided, because he wasn't going to show him. After the fuss he'd made in getting on that trip tomorrow, the last thing he wanted to do was call in sick. Today's snickers would become tomorrow's belly laughs. He'd never be able to show his face in the squadron again.

He made a command decision to ignore the pulsing bump. Bump, he repeated. A small one. Not in the goose-egg class at all.

Steam was fogging the mirror as he pushed open the door to the shower and stepped inside. The water was just a shade on the warm side. Third-degree burns he didn't need. With a curse, he turned the lever and ducked under the needle-sharp spray.

Hurry, he told himself, but couldn't help but linger as the tense reactions of the last few minutes melted into nothing. Jennifer was waiting, perhaps with a description of his attacker. He hoped not, because that meant she'd gotten close enough to see him.

He turned his face into the spray, wincing as the lump on his forehead reminded him of its presence. He was wondering if he'd be able to pull his flight cap on over it when he heard a persistent knocking on the shower door.

"Matt? I need to talk to you."

He smiled. Lovely, gentle Jennifer. Making herself confront him in the shower to prove his nudity didn't faze her. Such sweet innocence. "Yes, Jennifer?" he said, realigning the spray before sliding the door open a few inches. "What is it that can't wait until we're both dressed?"

She kept her eyes averted and mumbled something he couldn't hear. Reaching out a dripping hand, he lifted her chin until her gaze met his, albeit reluctantly. "Say that again, sweet. It's hard to hear with the shower going."

She swallowed, then took a deep breath. "There's something you need to know about what happened."

His brows drew together as he considered the worry in her expression. The diversions hadn't worked after all. She was blaming herself for not catching the guy. He tried for a tone of firm consolation. "It's not your fault he got away, sweet. You'll notice I didn't do anything to catch him." He grinned and planted a wet kiss on her forehead. "If the truth be known, I'm not sure I would have given chase even if I'd been able to. Chasing bad guys doesn't seem worth the risks." His hand dropped from her chin as he waited for his words of reason to prevail.

"Would you shut up and let me get in a word edgewise!"

If her command didn't exactly sink in, the fire in her eyes gave him pause. Matt stared at his sweet, innocent little Jennifer and wondered where the sweet and innocent parts had disappeared to.

The woman standing in his bathroom was roaring mad.

"You're such a bloody chauvinist sometimes, I can hardly bear it. Didn't you imagine for even one second there was no 'guy' or 'attacker'?"

Chauvinist? Him? She must be misinterpreting what he'd said. Matt shook his head slowly. "No, I never imagined there wasn't an attacker. I didn't just jump into the hot tub headfirst, now did I?"

"Did it never occur to you that it was a 'gal' and not a 'guy'?"

Again, he shook his head, still puzzled by the outraged expression on her face. "It took a pretty hefty blow to knock me off my feet—"

"You were on your knees, Colonel!" she yelled, then took several angry breaths as she made an obvious attempt to calm herself. "And it didn't take much effort at all. You're not invincible just because you outweigh me by a few pounds."

"More like seventy or eighty—" It hit him then, the thing she'd been too embarrassed to tell him. And it hadn't been embarrassment at all, but *guilt. Pure, well-deserved guilt.* A wave of something totally outrageous surged through him. He touched the tennis-ball-sized lump on his forehead and made a show of wincing. "You could have killed me!"

"That's what you get for showing up where you don't belong!"

"Don't belong!" he bellowed, slamming his hand on the wall. "This is my house—"

"And you're supposed to be on some secret mission, Colonel." Her jaw was clenched so tightly he was amazed it didn't crack. But when she started yelling at him again, he figured she'd done that just to distract him.

"How was I to know that 'guy' I saw bending over the hot tub"—she put an emphasis on *guy* that he didn't like—"wasn't going to break into the house?"

"After he finished cleaning the hot tub, I suppose." Matt deliberately didn't yell. Between the tennis-ball-sized lump on his forehead and the excellent acoustics of the shower stall, his head was beginning to throb.

Her jaw started working again. "This wouldn't have happened if you had let me know you were home."

He shut off the shower and threw open the door, forcing Jennifer to back off or get trampled. She made a good choice and went to sit on the toilet. Her first good choice of the day, he judged.

"A burglar could have stripped this place clean—including the papa-san chair—and you would have slept right through it." He grabbed a towel and dried himself without worrying about her sensibilities. Jennifer embarrassed by his nudity? What a laugh!

She muttered something that sounded like "no big loss" but Matt was rubbing the towel over his hair and couldn't be sure.

"I would have heard if someone had broken in," she said in a voice that was much quieter than her previous bellow. "The doors were locked, in case you didn't notice. I'm not a complete idiot."

The absurdity of their argument finally got to him. Dropping the towel, he turned to face her. "I didn't mean what I said about the burglar. I'm sure you would have caught him before he got to the stereo equipment."

She eyed him suspiciously. "I really didn't know it was you."

"I know."

She seemed to believe him. "I didn't mean to call you a bloody chauvinist," she muttered.

He grinned. "Yes, you did." He hunkered down in front of her and held her gaze with his. "Do I really treat you like a helpless female?"

"Only half the time. When you're not thinking straight." She rested a hand on his shoulder, the warmth of her touch soothing his turbulent emotions. "I know you only want to protect me, Matt, but it seems like you take it a little far at times."

"Perhaps it's because I want you to rely on me." He covered her hand with his and brought it to his cheek. "You're such an independent little thing. Maybe I worry where I fit in your life."

"It's not a matter of where either of us fit." She slipped off the stool and knelt before him, between his thighs. "People who are planning permanent relationships have to think about stuff like that. We shouldn't waste our time. We have so little of it."

Her soft cotton sweatsuit was an erotic rub against the insides of his thighs, distracting him. She was good at that, he mused, staring into her calm, clear eyes.

"I'll make you a deal." He pulled her into his arms and held her close to his heart. "You quit reminding me that you're leaving someday, and I'll try to remember you're neither as innocent nor as helpless as you look."

She pushed back and gave him a worried look. "I look innocent?"

He laughed and tickled her ear with his mouth. "Don't make me lie, sweet. I've already made enough concessions today."

"Innocent?" she murmured, her hands finding his thighs and beginning a provocative exploration that made him realize he didn't know the meaning of the word.

His breath caught in his throat as she cupped him in her innocent hands, stroking his hard, pulsing length . . . proving once again that appearances were not only deceptive . . .

They were, at times, outright lies.

Twelve

"I thought you said you could cook." Matt smeared a dollop of peanut butter on a cracker and offered it to Jennifer. She was sitting on a high stool on the other side of the counter, looking suitably mussed and warm in his Seattle Seahawks sweatshirt, which fell nearly to her knees.

"I said I *liked* to cook." She popped the cracker into her mouth and chewed. Wiping a smudge of peanut butter from her lips, she gave him a mischievous grin. "I never claimed to be any good at it."

He eyed her suspiciously. "And just how often do you *like* to cook."

"Almost never."

"That doesn't sound like someone who likes to cook," he drawled. "'Almost never' sounds like someone who lied about it in the first place."

The expression on her face was deliberately innocent. "Trust me, Matt. This kitchen will stay much cleaner if we just agree that I *don't* cook."

"You don't cook." He nodded and looked around at the cabinets and appliances that were sparkling like new. "You clean rather nicely, I have to admit."

She beamed at his praise. "Now, that's something I can do. Wait till I get to the rest of the house. You won't recognize it." She stared at the pan into which he'd just dumped a can of soup and licked her lips.

"I'm so hungry that canned soup is making me drool. Do you think you can rush that a bit?"

So it was going to be more of "whatever you can fix on the barbecue" for the duration, Matt thought. Well, it wasn't like he was used to anything better. He checked the directions on the can of soup and added water to the pan. "You have only yourself to blame for this meal. Maybe next time you'll wait to attack me until after I've gotten something from the freezer."

Jennifer rested her elbows on the countertop and batted her lashes at him. "I told you we could defrost the steaks in the microwave. Isn't that what those machines are for?"

He shook his head and wondered how a nanny who couldn't cook managed to keep her charges from starving. "Every time I try that, I end up with shoe leather."

She nodded. "Well, it's a moot point anyway. Midnight is a bit late to be standing outside grilling steaks."

He grinned at her. "Again, sweet, that's your fault. We could have been downstairs by ten if you'd paid any attention to the signals my stomach was sending."

A hot flush colored her cheeks, but she recouped with grace. "Is that what those noises were? It was hard to hear them over all that moaning you were doing."

It was his turn to flush. "The moans were your fault too. Need I remind you what you were doing?"

She gulped and nibbled on her lower lip. "I think that could wait for after dinner, don't you?"

Barely. Matt allowed himself a single shudder of pleasure before putting a lid on the impulse to take her where she sat—on the stool, a quick, hot thrust into her wet core.

He was ready and willing.

He was also hungry.

He needed a spoon to stir the soup, and had to look

in four drawers before he found one. "Why'd you move the silverware?"

"Shelf paper. It was easier to move things from one place to another rather than empty and then refill each drawer."

He frowned, regarding her curiously. "Is that why the pots and pans are in the cabinet over the refrigerator now instead of where they belong?"

"I found them under the sink," she said dryly. "Convince me that's any better than where I put them."

They would have been in the cabinets under the counter where they belonged were it not for the collection of 45 records he'd stored there while he built extra shelves in the study—a project that he had yet to begin. Matt didn't dare check to see if his precious records were still there.

"You'll need a footstool to reach the pots clear up there," he pointed out, turning off the burner under the soup.

"Why should I need them at all?" she asked. She walked around the counter, dug in a low drawer, and came up with two bowls. "I don't cook, remember?"

Matt stared at the bowls. "Why did you put those in the bottom drawer?"

"These I'll use."

He flipped open an eye-level cabinet. Empty. "What's wrong with here?"

"Too high." She opened the dishwasher and pulled out a couple of napkins. He glimpsed the telephone book on the bottom rack before she slammed the door shut. "You built this place for a giant, you know."

He made up his mind to buy her a footstool the first chance he had. "Did it occur to you that those napkins will get wet in there?"

"Why should they?" Edging in front of him, she filled the bowls with soup, then carried them around the counter.

"Oh, I don't know." Matt tried to keep the skepticism out of his voice and failed. His wonderful, independent Jennifer was definitely out of her element in the kitchen. The thought pleased him because until now, she'd seemed almost too capable. "I guess I was thinking of using the machine for washing dishes. Silly me."

"I never use dishwashers. Doing them by hand relaxes me." She hopped back up on her stool and took a cautious taste of the soup. "It's a great place for the phone book, though. Have you ever noticed that the city directories keep getting thicker whereas the drawer where you're supposed to put the book is too full of other junk to fit it in?"

No, he hadn't. Matt spooned some soup into his mouth and went back to the cooking thing. "What did you feed Keith and Carrie if you can't cook?"

"Most of the time, they ate with their folks. When they didn't, we managed on macaroni and cheese, fish sticks, or frozen chicken pies. Kid food is different from people food. Boiling water is about as hard as it gets." She lifted the spoon to her mouth and blew on the hot soup. "I don't know what moms did before microwaves, though. Did you realize we could have heated this soup in there?"

"The last time I tried that, it took an hour to clean up the mess." Matt finished his soup and reached for another cracker. "How do I know you won't starve while I'm gone?"

"You're leaving?" Her spoon fell from her fingers, clattering against the nearly empty bowl. She took a deep breath, then turned on her stool to face him, her gaze clouded with confusion. "I thought your trip was canceled."

She thought that because that's what he'd told her to explain his sudden reappearance. The guilt he'd felt upon telling the lie had been eating at him ever since.

"I lied. There wasn't a trip today. It's tomorrow."

"But you left here this morning in your flight suit. After the phone call—"

He shook his head. "I went out to McChord and begged for a slot on the next trip. That's tomorrow evening. After that, I spent a couple of hours in the BOQs."

"BOQs?"

"Bachelor officer quarters. It's where we some-times stay when we're on trips. I had planned to spend the night there, but I changed my mind."

"But why couldn't you stay here, Matt? Is it me? Did you change your mind about wanting me to stay?" Her confusion had evolved into hurt, and that was the last thing he'd intended.

He took her small hands in his, bracketing her bare legs between his jeans-clad thighs. "I needed some space, Jennifer. I thought that if I could get away, I could learn to deal with some things a little easier."

She sucked her bottom lip between her teeth. "What things?"

To tell or not to tell? He could stick with what he'd decided that afternoon and keep her ignorant of the love he felt for her. It would be easier for her to leave, not realizing that she was taking his heart with her. Then again, what had lying earned him besides a dunking in the hot tub and a lump on his forehead?

He didn't want there to be any lies between them. Time was too short, too precious. And if Jennifer was as strong and independent as she claimed, what he felt shouldn't make a difference in her plans.

He wouldn't let it.

"I love you, Jennifer Delaney."

"Excuse me?" She blinked rapidly, her jaw drop-ping open in stunned disbelief.

"You heard me, sweet. I said I love you. I left to figure out what I was going to do about it." He pulled his gaze from hers, swallowing back the disappoint-ment at her obvious horror. Clearly, this wasn't what she wanted to hear.

He didn't feel real good about saying it, either.

Honesty wasn't all it was cracked up to be.

"You can't do that," she said.

"Do what?" He stared at the fluorescent light and thought its sterile brightness was appropriate to this dialogue. The soft, warm lights of romance would certainly be out of place.

"Love me, of course. You can't do that."

His gaze swung back to meet hers. "Why not?"

"Because I have places to go, things to do." She scooted off the stool and went to stand against the wall, her arms crossed over her breasts. "Falling in love wasn't part of the deal, Colonel."

He hated it when she called him that. "I didn't say anything about asking you to change your plans, now, did I?"

She glared at him suspiciously and shook her head.

"And I never will." He slid off his stool and closed the distance between them. "Tying you down wouldn't be fair to either of us. I've had my chance to see the world. I won't deny you yours."

Her stare drilled a hole in his chest. "This changes everything."

"It changes nothing." His fingers under her chin, he forced her head up until the full force of her angry glare seared through his eyes straight into his soul. "Do you really think I want to spend my life with a woman who has her heart somewhere in the outside world? I would never know if I'd wake up one morning and find you gone."

"If I said I would stay, I would do just that. Stay." She scowled. "You don't think much of my character, do you?"

He blinked a couple of times, thinking that perhaps she was getting off the subject. "Your character isn't in question, Jennifer. The fact that I love you shouldn't change your dreams, though. I wouldn't have told you at all if I thought it would."

She looked genuinely distressed, and a shiver that might have been fear visibly coursed through her. "But what if—"

He interrupted her before she could finish. This wasn't a time for what-ifs. "Don't be afraid, Jennifer. When it's time for you to go, I'll be there to give you a push out the door. There won't be anyone here holding you back from your dreams."

"I can take care of my dreams without your help," she said, clenching her jaw.

"I know you can. Just remember that I can take care of mine too. They aren't your responsibility."

The anger in her gaze faded, only to be replaced by a regret so deep, he almost wished the anger was back. "You said I was afraid." She gulped and took a ragged breath. "I'm not afraid, Matt. I know I can leave when I'm ready. But I don't want to hurt you either."

"If you leave now, you'll wound me for life." He put his hands flat against the wall on either side of her head. "I've never known anyone like you, Jennifer. I need more time."

"We both do," she said softly. "I told you once before. When I leave, it will be when something is over between us . . . and not before it's even begun."

He swallowed hard and smiled down at her. "I think we've made a good beginning, sweet."

She nodded, her eyes rounding in serious deliberation. "This thing between us. How can it ever be over when one of us has gone and fallen in love?"

"You'll know when it's over, Jennifer. It will be your call."

"A few months? Will that be enough?"

"A week, a month. Or more." He shrugged. "It depends on how fast that agency comes up with a job for you. I won't have you sticking around when something irresistible comes along."

She put her hands on his shoulders and raised up on her toes, brushing her mouth across his chin. "There's one thing you haven't considered."

He lowered his head to touch her lips with his. "And what's that, sweet?"

"What if I fall in love with you? Wouldn't it make sense to stay here and not leave at all?"

He denied her speculation with a shake of his head, even as his heart thumped crazily at the sheer pleasure of such a thing ever happening. Bittersweet pleasure, though, because it would make no difference in the end.

How could her love—should that ever happen, which he doubted—withstand the crushing of her dreams?

"Not even then, Jennifer. You've had your dream too long to give up on it now. I won't let you." He pressed his lips to hers and was surprised by the slight tremble in the kiss she returned. "Besides, you wouldn't fall in love with a decrepit pilot who's nearly twice your age, now, would you?"

"You're not twice my age." She shifted her stance subtly, and the anxiety of the last few minutes was gone, replaced by another kind of tension that was kinder, more familiar. Jennifer wrapped her hands around his neck and tried to deepen the kisses that were heated interludes between half-spoken pleas. "You're not that old at all, even though you act like it sometimes. Did I ever tell you I find older men attractive?"

He opened her mouth under his and took a long, luxurious taste of the honeyed sweetness he found there. "Change that to older 'man' and I won't turn you over my knee."

She giggled and poked her tongue in his ear, earning one of those moans he gave so easily when she teased him. "You're fun, Matt. You make me laugh. I have to admit that I do like being with you."

"That's not saying much." He slipped his hands under her knees and held her to his chest as he carried her into the living room. "You liked being with Keith and Carrie. They probably made you laugh, too."

"I do enjoy making love with you," she went on as though to herself. "I think I should miss that a lot."

"Don't understate the facts, sweet. We're dynamite together."

"And we do seem to have a lot to talk about." She leaned back in his arms to stare up at him. "I've never felt so comfortable with anyone before."

"When you're not kicking me around, I suppose I could say the same thing."

She touched his forehead with her fingers. "Next time, call before you come back. It's probably less risky that way."

"You'll stay for a while then?" He hadn't been sure, had wanted to kick his own butt for even starting this conversation.

But he'd had to tell her. It wasn't something he would have been able to hide for much longer. As he'd said, they were dynamite together. In the explosion of their passion, who could have blamed him for sharing with her what was in his heart? It was better that she hear it now, when they could deal with it logically.

"So you'll stay, Jennifer? You won't hold it against me if I've been a bit careless with my heart?"

She ignored his question.

"You make me feel safe, Colonel Cooper," she said, her expression suddenly serious. "Happy and satisfied and entertained and safe. People have been known to stay together with fewer excuses than that."

His arms tightened around her as he tried to keep her words in perspective. She was just trying to make him feel better. He pasted a smile on his face and kept his tone light. "You sound like you're trying to talk yourself into something." He kissed the tip of her nose. "Don't worry about it, sweet. It's my problem. I can take care of it when the time comes."

"When the time comes," she whispered. Avoiding his gaze, she looked around the room from her perch in his arms. He should let her down, he knew, but really, she weighed hardly anything.

He figured he could hold her another five minutes before his arms started to shake.

"You do have a really nice house, Matt."

"Thank you."

"Have you ever considered letting a professional decorator have a look at it?"

"What do I need with a decorator? I've got plenty of

things, enough furniture for the whole house." He managed to hold on to her as he turned in a complete circle. "Everything here is from one trip or another. It's comfortable. I like it."

"Oh, dear."

His gaze sharpened on her. "What do you mean by that?"

"Honestly?"

He nodded, keeping his reservations to himself. This honesty thing was getting out of hand.

She wiggled out of his arms and went to stand by the papa-san chair. "To begin with, the flowers on this cushion clash with the carpet and the drapes."

"So change the drapes. I don't pay much attention to stuff like that."

"Obviously." Her smile took the sting out of her comment. "I don't mean you have to get rid of the chair. I do think, though, it would look better in the game room downstairs. Did you realize you've got a perfectly beautiful sofa down there that would look spectacular in this room?"

"I like the papa-san chair up here. It's comfortable."

"For one, maybe." She clasped her hands behind her back. "What do you do when you want to cuddle with someone in front of that incredible view? The papa-san chair is so . . . limiting."

He pushed his thumbs through his belt loops. "There's room for both of us in the chair, sweet."

She shook her head. "The rattan isn't strong enough to hold all that weight. I'm surprised it doesn't fall apart when you sit in it all by yourself."

"It wouldn't dare."

She acknowledged his boast with a grin. "I can tell this isn't going to be easy."

"What isn't going to be easy?"

"Getting you to rearrange the furniture." She pointed at the antler and horsehair footstool. "I suppose you have a soft spot for that atrocity."

"Atrocity?" He was wounded. Deeply. "I found that

at an auction in the English countryside. It's an antique."

"It's a dreadful example of how far people will go to make a buck." She shuddered and walked over to where the peacock feathers adorned the hearth. "These are nice, Matt. They'd look lovely next to the pinball machine in the basement."

"What's wrong with where they are?"

She winced and shook her head. "Never mind. I shouldn't have let myself get carried away. But you told me to be honest."

He stared at her for a long moment before crossing to her. "You really get a kick out of this kind of thing, don't you?"

"I told you before. I like making a house feel like a home." She went easily into his embrace, her own arms sliding around his back. "You've got some wonderful furniture and things, Matt. Well, most of it is wonderful. That footstool is really something else."

"I suppose I could always give it to Rick. He's got a matching coffee table."

Her shoulders shook as she laughed. He hugged her closer, thinking that if they never moved from this spot, that life would go on without them, that Jennifer would never leave . . .

He shut his eyes against the pain.

"It really excites me," she said, "to imagine how this house could look if I just rearranged things a bit."

"I guess I just buy what I like. It never occurred to me to worry about how it goes together." Well, not really. But then, he wasn't about to admit that he'd deliberately rearranged the furniture for her benefit.

"I suppose if it's that bad . . ." He let his words linger in the air, taking perverse pride in the wounded tone he'd managed. He'd make her feel guilty, just for a moment, then she could do whatever she pleased. As long as it made her happy, he didn't care if she chucked the papa-san chair into the hot tub.

Maybe a good dunking would tighten up the sagging rattan.

She looked up at him, a frown creasing her forehead. "I didn't mean to criticize, Matt. It's just that I have a knack for putting things together. You're a pilot. You shouldn't have to worry about things like which curtains go with what chair in which room."

"Pilots don't have to have any taste? Is that what you're implying?"

"Don't be so touchy, Matt. I just think that pilots have enough to worry about, what with defying the laws of gravity every time they go to work." She gave an enormous sigh. "It scares me to death knowing what goes up must come down. I'm always afraid it will come down much too fast."

Was this the same woman who had considered hang gliding as an adventure? He pushed his hand into the hair at her nape and brought her face back to his chest. "Will you make love with me in the papa-san chair before it gets moved?"

"Not even once." She punched him in the side. "I told you I wanted adventure in my life, not unadulterated danger."

He laughed and made up his mind to show her the chair wasn't nearly as unstable as she imagined. He hoped. He'd do it later, though, after he'd gotten his fill of just holding her.

Their hearts beat together in a slow, easy cadence that made holding her all the more appealing. Erratic, exciting rhythms were fine during lovemaking. Essential, unavoidable. He'd never think of her and not remember those glorious, exhilarating explosions of passion. But he needed the quiet memories too.

He touched his lips to her hair, drinking in the fragrance that was so essentially Jennifer. "You can rearrange things to your heart's content, sweet. I don't mind as long as you don't try to lift anything too heavy."

She twisted her neck to look up at him. "You're

sure, Matt? You're not just trying to give me something to do?"

He suddenly thought of the disorganized tangle she'd made of the kitchen and wondered what his house would resemble when she got done with it. "Do what you like, Jennifer. If you've got any ideas that cost money, write them down and we'll discuss them when I get back."

The excitement in her eyes was a reward like none other. "I won't throw away anything without asking you first."

"Good."

"And if you don't like it, we can always move things back to where they were."

"Agreed." Turning her in his arms, he led her toward the papa-san chair.

"When do you leave?" she asked.

"Tomorrow evening." He bent down and kissed her neck. "Since I'll have to spend tomorrow afternoon resting up before the mission, what do you say we stay up late tonight?"

Her eyebrows lifted in amusement. "Is there a fantasy we haven't fulfilled, Matt?"

He tumbled her into the papa-san chair and followed her down, crushing her into the deep, soft cushion. "A million of them, Jennifer. At least a million."

Her eyes were wide and sparkling with life. "When this chair falls apart, Matt, at least that will be one problem solved."

He covered her sassy mouth with his and kissed her hard enough to drive that blasphemous thought right out of her mind.

Thirteen

Over coffee the next morning, Matt was quick to point out that the papa-san chair had survived. Admirably. Jennifer just waggled her fingers and gave him a look that he interpreted to mean the chair's future hadn't been secured.

He kept his worries to himself and offered her a selection of activities for the morning. They could take advantage of the glorious weather and go sailing for a few hours. Or would she like to try a spot of bungee jumping?

Bungee jumping? Did he think she was mad? For that matter, she couldn't picture him flinging himself off a ledge or out of a balloon to bounce upside down in midair until the spring went out of the bungee. His gray hairs would multiply and fall out before he could get the bungee cord off his heels.

He grinned and said he was only offering the activity. He was not intending to participate. Not that he'd really thought she'd go through with it, he admitted. Anyone who had put hang gliding in the "best left for others" category was not likely to seek the thrills of bungee jumping.

He'd just wanted to make sure she knew there was plenty of excitement to be had in the Pacific Northwest. Enough to keep her busy for months.

Months, she agreed. It would take at least that

long to get another nanny job. In the meantime, there was the matter of finding something local. Would Matt mind if she made a few calls about the ads she'd seen in the paper?

Yes, he minded. It could wait one more day, until he was gone.

They ended up taking a drive down to the post office, where Jennifer picked up an assortment of boxes from Pilau and Montana. Arriving home, she started to put the clothes away in the guest room before Matt stopped her.

My room, he insisted. Our room. That's where your things belong.

She didn't argue, not then, or later when he picked her up and dropped her onto the bed. A nap was essential, and he didn't want to sleep alone.

He didn't know which one of them was more surprised when they woke up four hours later, having done nothing more than sleep. In a controlled rush, Matt showered, dressed, and tucked a handful of clean clothes in his bag.

The five minutes he saved by rushing was spent in more important pursuits, like kissing Jennifer. Saying good-bye. Wishing he didn't have to leave at all.

She proved she was stronger than he by pushing him out the door when he'd almost forgotten he had a reason for leaving. He left, watching her in the rearview mirror as he drove down the street, her hand raised in a motionless wave.

Sweet, gentle Jennifer, he thought as he turned toward the interstate.

The papa-san chair didn't stand a chance.

Matt waited his turn for the long-distance line in base ops. The rest of the crew had already made their "it was a close one but we made it" calls.

Yes, it had been close. A hatch had blown out after takeoff from Dover Air Force Base in Delaware. At twenty-eight thousand feet, everything that hadn't been tied down had been sucked out by the rapid decompression, an emergency he'd drilled for but had never experienced.

It hadn't been fun. The air had condensed in a second, filling the cabin and cockpit with a freezing mist as the aircrew pulled on oxygen masks and tried to keep the aircraft stable in the congested traffic that was normal for New York airspace. The emergency turnaround, the fuel dump over the Atlantic, and the subsequent landing had all been accomplished with cool precision.

Only then had Matt begun to sweat. They'd been lucky. No one had been hurt, with the exception of an airman who'd been bopped on the head by debris of some sort on its way out the hatch. Everyone considered that minor, though, because if the crew hadn't still been strapped into their seats, the losses might have been more than blankets, miscellaneous boxes, and the spare ladder to the flight deck.

It was sure to make the news back in Tacoma. The local paper tended to follow stories regarding McChord-based crews and planes.

Matt needed to call Jennifer before she read the paper. He picked up the phone and punched in his home number. When she didn't answer until the fifth ring, he knew she'd been fast asleep. Considering it was two A.M. her time, he wasn't surprised.

"'Lo?"

"Jennifer, it's me. Matt."

"Hmm." He could almost see her snuggling deeper into the pillows with the phone smashed against her ear. "I'm 'sleep."

He sighed and wished he could have waited until later. He couldn't, though, because they were getting ready to take off again. Now that the emergency was over, they had to ferry the aircraft up to McGuire Air Force Base in New Jersey for repairs. He wouldn't have another chance to call until the paper was on her doorstep.

"I know you're asleep, sweet. I just needed to call and tell you something. So you wouldn't worry."

Silence greeted his words, so he plunged in, giving her the bare details.

"Not worried," she answered. "The papa-san chair can be fixed with a little glue. And I found some terrific fabric that will blend with the curtains in the game room."

"Papa-san chair?" What did that have to do with rapid decompression?

"Mm-hm. And the scratches on the wall won't show at all once I get that wallpaper up."

"What wall?" He needn't have been concerned about her getting upset with his news. Jennifer wasn't worried. She wasn't even awake.

"The white one." He heard her yawn clear across the country.

"What did you do to the papa-san chair, Jennifer?" As if he couldn't guess.

"Didn't do anything. It fell all by itself."

He didn't want to know how far or where. "As long as you're not worried, sweet. Now why don't you go back to sleep."

"Am asleep," she mumbled, then yawned again. "Matt?"

"Yes, love?"

"What are you doing in New York?"

So she'd been listening after all.

Matt was three days and eleven thousand miles late coming home.

It was midmorning when he let himself into the house, an empty house. Jennifer wasn't home. When they'd talked earlier—he'd called her from base ops upon landing, an appropriate precaution given his respect for Jennifer's welcome-home kicks—she'd told him she had a job interview at eleven, then another at two. Both were with day-care centers, and she was crossing her fingers for luck. They would celebrate with a barbecue that night, he said, turning a deaf ear to her qualms that success wouldn't necessarily be hers. But she'd promised to get the steaks out of the freezer, just in case.

Lugging his bag up the stairs, Matt took a brief shower and fell onto the bed for a nap, his dreams filled with the woman whose scent clung to the pillows and sheets. When he awakened a few hours later, he showered again and pulled on jeans and his pink cotton sweater that was a particular favorite of Jennifer's. It made him look sexy, she'd said, without explaining why pink was a sexy color.

He'd have to take her with him the next time he needed to buy clothes, he thought. Her tastes in clothes reflected the woman she was—decisive and unpredictable.

It was the unpredictable part that made Matt hurry down the stairs to the living room. He was a couple yards into the room before the truth of what he was looking at sank in.

Nothing.

No papa-san chair. Nor horsehair and antlers footstool. No peacock feathers or china elephant. And that wasn't all that was missing.

There wasn't a single stick of furniture in the entire room. It was as bare as the day the builder had walked out the door for the last time. Paint, carpet, a brick heath, and brass inset fireplace.

There weren't even any curtains.

The thought that he'd been robbed flashed through his mind, followed by the codicil that having Jennifer in his house hadn't made it theft-proof after all.

Both thoughts were disposed of as he realized a thief wouldn't have bothered with curtains.

"Damn that woman," he muttered, walking across the barren room and noticing there wasn't a speck of dust to be found either. "I told her not to carry anything heavy."

No wonder the papa-san chair had suffered a slight fracture. She'd probably dropped it down the basement stairs.

He turned on his heel and descended the staircase

to the basement, not missing the scratches that paralleled the railing. He paused on the bottom step and surveyed what had once been a spacious game room.

It was stuffed with everything from upstairs, including the papa-san chair, which was tilting sadly.

He wondered if she planned on leaving it that way.

He really didn't mind. Keeping Jennifer busy was just another way of keeping her happy, he mused as he walked back upstairs. Although where she expected him to sit in the meantime was a question he intended to put to her when she came home.

Which should be anytime now. He checked his watch, then walked outside to the mailbox. Sifting through the miscellaneous personal and occupant-addressed letters, he found one for Jennifer.

From something called "Nannies Abroad."

He was filled with a kind of dread that he knew would eventually disappear . . . only to be replaced by something equally intolerable.

Emptiness.

Matt was grilling onions in a skillet when Jennifer let herself in from the garage. He forced a smile and held out one arm. She came to him without a moment's hesitation, burying herself against his side, her arms twining around him in a hold that felt like she was determined never to let go.

It was a fantasy that would never become real.

He dropped a kiss on her forehead and gave her a quick squeeze with the one arm. The other he deliberately kept busy with the onions. "I missed you, too, sweet."

She let go of him long enough to snatch the fork from his fingers and lift the skillet off the burner. Batting her long, gorgeous eyelashes at him, she shimmied against him in a move that made him all hard and soft at the same time, like melted wax. She melted him with fire and made him burn.

"You're all words and no actions, flyboy. Why don't you show me you really mean it."

Lord, but when she was this close, it was impossible not to do exactly that. He'd intended to be casual with her, aloof even.

Letting go was going to be harder then he'd ever imagined. Perhaps it was the timing, he mused as he put both arms around her and hauled her tight against his body. They'd had days, not months. So much less than either had expected.

There was no changing the letter, though. His big hands closed around her tush, pulling her up onto her toes, fitting her to where she fitted best. He found her mouth open and hungry to his kiss. She was aggressive, impatient almost.

Matt was just plain desperate. The turmoil of his emotions must have communicated itself to her, because she pulled back from his embrace and stared at him with a curiosity that was part teasing part fear.

"Matt? What's wrong?"

He knew he had to get it over with. Bitter medicine was like that. The faster, the better.

He reached past her to the stove and set the skillet back onto the burner. "There's a letter for you. Over there, on the counter."

Horror filled her expression, but was gone in an instant—so fast that he could almost imagine he hadn't seen it at all. "You picked up the mail?"

He nodded. "It's from Nannies Abroad. I assume that's the agency that sent you to Pilau."

"Yes, but—"

"Just open it, Jennifer. Get it over with. Please." Before he went out of his mind.

She turned away so swiftly, her hair swung out in an arc that cut across his arm, her special scent filling the air despite the onions. He kept his gaze on the stove and his back to the counter.

It was like preparing to be shot in the back, he mused. But he didn't have the strength to turn around and watch as she opened the letter to her future.

Without him.

He heard the tear as she ripped open the envelope, the crackle of heavy bond paper. Even her unsteady breathing was audible above the pop and crackle of the onions.

Or was it his breathing?

"Kuwait." She sounded relieved, and he couldn't understand why. He'd been to Kuwait. So had Saddam Hussein. Big deal.

He turned off the burner and lifted the skillet aside, taking his time as he tried to assemble his emotions into something more supportive than resentful anger. When he faced her, he leaned back against the counter with his arms folded across his chest. She stared right back at him, folding the paper in her hands into a tiny square.

"Kuwait?" he finally asked, unable to do anything about the scowl on his face. "Not exactly a garden spot, but certainly exotic-sounding." There. That was as positive as he could get. He would have been proud of the effort were it not for what it cost him.

His heart.

"It's also right at the bottom of my list," she said, "somewhere around racing down a bobsled track and eating sushi." Shoving the letter into the pocket of her skirt, she leaned back against the opposite counter, imitating his stance right down to the crossed arms and scowl. "I've never been that interested in desert landscapes."

His heart beat with the springy flutter of hope. "You're not eager to try sushi?"

"I prefer to think of it as keeping an open mind for the time being. When I get past everything else on the list—about the time I turn eighty, I figure—I'm sure I'll get up enough nerve to give it a try." She sucked her bottom lip between her teeth, nibbling on it as she looked at him. "There's always the possibility that sushi will go out of style by then."

"Kuwait will still be there."

"Probably. Matt I never said anything about taking the first job that was offered.

"I was expecting the worst." He swallowed over the lump in his throat. "I'm not ready for you to go."

"And I'm not ready to leave." Her arms fell to her sides as she walked to him. Prying his own arms from his chest, she placed them around her waist, then looked up at him with a stare that was so hot and hungry, he felt himself harden and pulse with need.

"So what do you say, flyboy? Do you think you can give me a proper greeting this time?"

He growled deep in his throat as his fingers undid the zipper at the back of her skirt. "I'll show you ready, sweet."

In the end, they showed each other, coming together with a reckless speed that would have been dangerous had he not remembered at that last, vital second the protection in the drawer in his bedroom. Cursing and muttering, he swept up her partially clad body and raced with her up the stairs.

"You might begin to do your part," he said, "and carry one of those little packets around in your purse. I won't always have the strength to carry you upstairs, you know."

She laughed and tickled his ear with her tongue. "If you'd given me the chance, I would have told you about what I hid in the drawer under the telephone."

"Under the phone?" He gave a surprised chuckle, then tossed her onto the bed and reached into the bedside table.

There was a method to her madness, he admitted. Finding his place between her thighs, he wondered how long it would take him to figure it out.

And then, Matt thought no more.

He savored her touch, her warmth.

He delighted in her sensual appeal, her innocence.

He reached for the stars . . . and found a piece of heaven with the angel in his arms.

Heaven became hell with one swift kick, Jennifer-style. Decisive and unpredictable.

He'd left her in bed, returning downstairs to light the coals in the grill. He paused in the kitchen to pick up their discarded clothes. A piece of paper fell from the pocket of her skirt. The letter, he realized. Curious as to what kind of enticement they'd offer in exchange for a year in the desert, he unfolded the paper and held it up to light. His gaze skimmed over what appeared to be a standard form, flitting to the bottom where he found terms, conditions, and bonuses.

His heart skipped a beat when he saw the country of destination: New Zealand.

Not Kuwait, but New Zealand. A beautiful country of mountains and lakes, sleepy villages and gorgeous beaches, both rocky and sandy. A paradise.

He should know. He'd been there.

Jennifer had lied. And Matt knew he couldn't let her get away with it.

New Zealand was too close to her dream to let it get away from her. Too beautiful, too exciting . . . too damned essential to a woman who wanted to see the world.

"Matt?"

He hadn't heard her. His entire body stiffened, as he turned to find her standing in the doorway, one of his squadron T-shirts almost making her decent. He could see shadows behind the inadequate veil of cotton, shadows with which he was well acquainted.

She looked rumpled and sleepy and generally well loved. He squeezed his eyes shut and took a deep breath. In the near silence that filled the air, he knew she'd seen the letter in his hands. The tiny sound she made was what a wounded animal might make after the initial shock had passed.

She hurt, and he would have to hurt her more.

He opened his eyes. She looked worse than she'd sounded. Pain filled her expression, and he thought he saw tears welling at the corners of her eyes.

"I wasn't prying, sweet. I was just curious."

"That's not important." Her voice was small and

deflated. It was as though she knew what was coming.

They both knew.

"You can't turn this down, Jennifer. I won't let you."

She wet her lips, her hands grabbing the hem of the T-shirt and tugging at it self-consciously. "It doesn't matter what the letter says, Matt. I'm not ready to go. Not yet."

He would have given his life to let her stay, but he couldn't.

A chance like this might never come her way again. The agency might take offense that she'd turned down a plum assignment like New Zealand. They might not offer her anything near as nice the next time.

Besides, he told himself, with each day she was with him, he got a little more used to her. There had been so few days, yet he knew already that with every day that passed, it would be harder to let her go.

"You can't turn this down, sweet. It doesn't make sense."

She shook her head emphatically. "I haven't been here—"

"Long enough," he interrupted. "Why don't you let this be my decision? You've already made a place for yourself in my heart. All another few months will do is make me bleed when you leave."

She looked terrified. "But you said—"

He cut her off again. "I said a lot of things that don't matter anymore. You've got this offer now, and I have my own life to put back together." He glanced over her shoulder toward the empty living room. "I've even got a living room to decorate, it seems. Nothing like a project to take my mind off . . ." His words trailed away as he focused again on her.

"Off you," he added softly, a reluctant smile edging his lips upward. "I'll never forget you, Jennifer. You brought something very special into my life."

"I don't want to go." Her words trembled into the air between them. "I'm not ready."

He suppressed the need to agree with her. "And I told you that I'd push you out that door when the time came." He steeled his resolve and moved toward her. Lifting a hand, he brushed the hair back from her forehead before cupping her chin. "It's time, sweet. And I'm pushing."

The tears welled, then tracked down her cheeks. "And I told you I didn't need any help following my dream."

"So you lied too." He kissed her eyelids shut, not able to look into her eyes any longer and do what needed to be done. "The letter says that if you want the job, you have to be ready to leave in a week. Would you like me to take leave from the squadron and spend that week with you?"

Her eyes flew open, and he saw a hopelessness there that he couldn't begin to deal with. He was casting about for something to say that would alleviate her hurt when she took a deep, fortifying breath and shook off his touch.

She looked at him, ignoring the tears that were rolling down her face. "That won't be necessary, Colonel. I'm sure you have better things to do."

"Nonsense!" His knuckles brushed away a track of tears, but it did no good. More fell before he could dry his hand. "I want to spend the time with you."

"And maybe I have better things to do, Colonel—"

"*Don't call me that!*" The air was turning cold, just like the blood inside him. She was distancing herself . . . and she wasn't even gone.

She sniffled and rubbed her fist across her eyes. "I think I'll go back home and see Charlie before I leave. He'll be glad of my company."

"But I want you to stay here." The magic week was suddenly shrinking to nothing.

"And I think I should catch the first plane for Montana. I don't suppose you could call the airlines and find me a flight home." She saw his stunned gaze and shook her head. "No, I didn't think so. I'll do it upstairs."

"Jennifer, don't—"

But he was speaking to her back. She'd already turned to run away and up the stairs.

He would have followed her, were it not for one thing.

Jennifer was doing what she had to do.

She was leaving.

Fourteen

Matt must have stared at the empty staircase a full ten minutes before turning back to the stove. He inspected the onions without any interest and threw the congealing mass into the garbage. The steaks he put into the refrigerator, along with the head of lettuce and other vegies he'd intended for their salad. It took a thirty-second trip outside to cover the grill and begin the slow death of the glowing coals.

So much for dinner.

He was standing in the middle of the kitchen without any idea of what to do next when he heard footsteps on the stairs.

Foot stomping, he corrected himself. There was nothing light or graceful about the thuds that signaled Jennifer's descent. He looked up to find her still dressed in his T-shirt and glaring at him with all the fury of a woman scorned.

A woman scorned? Now what had given him that idea? He peered closer and decided it was just plain fury.

Jennifer was mad as hell.

He'd heard of women who were beautiful in their anger, but that wasn't a primary focus at the moment. Jennifer was mad and nothing else came into the equation.

He wondered what had put her in this state.

Hands on hips, her bare feet planted in an aggressive stance that he worried might have something to do with her martial-arts training, she stared at him and huffed.

Actually huffed. He couldn't remember seeing anyone do that before.

She did it well.

"I'm not going." She spoke clearly and distinctly, as if to a deaf mute.

He still had trouble understanding. "You'll stay the week?"

Her fury jumped a notch. She was now as close to rage as he ever wanted to see her.

"I'll stay as long as I want. A week, a month . . . forever. It's my decision." She took a deep, harsh breath. "If that's what I want to do, I should be able to make that choice."

"Forever?" What the hell was she talking about? She had places to go, people to meet—

"Forever, dammit!" She crossed the floor and stood toe to toe with a man who wouldn't cross that invisible line if his life depended on it. "It's *my* decision and *I'm* going to make the choices. Not you. *Me.*"

"But—"

Her eyes blazed with green fire. "I got a job today. A *good* job. Not just something to get by on, but a job I really, really want."

"Tacoma isn't Pilau or New Zealand." She was missing the point. "It costs a lot of money to travel overseas. Don't you think having your way paid would be the easiest—"

"So what!" She pushed a wave of hair from her eyes with fingers that trembled. "I'm sick and tired of you making my decisions for me, Colonel. Did it ever occur to you that I might have a mind of my own?"

Well, yes, but then, he didn't want an unhappy woman in his bed for the rest of their lives.

He tried a gentle smile to soothe her. It didn't work. She glared back and inched forward, her hands fisted at her sides.

She gritted her teeth. He could actually hear her grinding away an appalling amount of enamel.

"You can be or stay wherever you want, Jennifer," he said carefully. "But you might never get to New Zealand that way."

"Damn New Zealand!"

He caught the first glimpse of tears since she'd come down from his room. Their room. "It's a nice place," he said weakly. "I should know. I've been there."

"And what's stopping you from going there again? With me!"

"Well, nothing, I suppose, but I'm not sure when—"

"I don't *care* when."

Her voice turned plaintive all of a sudden. Wistful. "Don't you understand, Colonel? New Zealand just wouldn't be the same without you."

What was she saying?

Matt was momentarily distracted from pursuing that line of thought when he felt her toes twitch against his. Did Jennifer know how ticklish he was? When her toes climbed over his, he was forced to gulp back an inappropriate laugh. He was considering a tactical retreat of a couple of inches when she grabbed his shoulders for balance and stepped right onto the tops of his feet.

Her ascent closed the footlong gap between them by three inches. When she rose up on her toes, there were less than six inches between their noses. Laughter was the last thing on his mind now as he felt her warm body sliding against his.

Her breasts brushed his chest, her breath sweetened the air between them as he cautiously circled her waist with his hands. His long fingers settled there, lightly though, because he wanted the initiative to be hers.

Just as the decision was hers. He knew that now.

Too bad he hadn't realized that before. It was odd, because he'd always considered himself to be a quick learner.

Jennifer threw him off center in more ways than one. From the moment they'd met, he'd been out of his depth.

Loving her had obviously slowed his thought process.

She planted a soft, gentle kiss on his chin. "I love you, Lieutenant Colonel Matt Cooper. I don't want to leave you. Not now. Not ever."

His breath wedged in his throat as he stared into her eyes—clear, honest eyes that were filled with love that was as unconditional as it was irrevocable.

She loved him. He hadn't dared hope for a miracle of that magnitude.

His fingers tightened around her waist. "Why is it I'm just now hearing about this?"

She gave a shy smile. "I didn't mention it before?"

"Not that I recall." He took a deep breath and let the truth fill him. She loved him.

He bent his head so their lips were nearly touching. "Do you remember when I warned you that falling in love wouldn't change anything?"

Panic flared in her eyes. She nodded.

"I was wrong."

Her eyes closed for a moment. When they flickered open again, they were filled with relief and love and even a few tears. He kissed away the tears and slid his arms all the way around her.

"I'm not going to press my luck by asking if you're sure about this," he said, his lips brushing her ear.

Her chest swelled as she took a deep breath. "We need to get a couple of things straight, Colonel."

"Matt." He pinched her butt without loosening his embrace, and smiled at her indignant squeal. "You're marrying the man, not the uniform."

"But I like the uniform," she began before taking a quick, startled breath. "Marrying?" She pushed back in his arms so that she could see his face.

He nodded. "My biological clock is ticking faster every day."

"Men don't have biological clocks."

"This one does." He leaned forward and kissed her

with slow, deliberate intent. "I want a family before I get much older, Jennifer. Do you think we could manage that in the next five or six years?"

"After five or six years, I think I might be ready." She slid her tongue across her lips and regarded him seriously. "How many generals have to worry about changing diapers?"

The image made him laugh. "Actually, I've been thinking about retiring from the air force before much longer."

"Retire? Matt, darling, you've go to do something about this hang-up you've got about your age." Her hair flew about her face as she shook her head in frustration. "You're not that old, trust me. Forty-three is barely out of your teens."

He grinned. "I'm just going to retire from the air force, Jennifer. I've earned the twenty-year pension, and I find there are other things I'd like to do—not quit working altogether. It's not too late for a midlife career change." Finding her waist with his hands again, he lifted her and settled her on the counter, wedging her legs apart so that he could stand between them.

Home.

"What kind of job?" Her hands linked behind his neck.

He shrugged, warming his hands on the firm satin of her thighs.

"I've been a nonflying partner in a local corporate jet service for about ten years now. I might decide to get in on the flying part of it."

"That's certainly an option." Her breathing quickened as his hands moved under the T-shirt, inching closer to the part of her that was open for his exploration.

He took his time, enjoying watching the signs of passion in her expression.

He would never get enough of her. Never. "Do you think that new job of yours will allow time for a vacation once in a while?"

"That's the beauty of it, Matt." Her eyes sparkled

with an enthusiasm that was infectious. "It's a job share in a private preschool with another woman. We share the same job and just coordinate our hours. With a little planning, I can take weeks off at a time."

"It's a good job?"

She nodded enthusiastically, then gulped as his touch neared her center. "It's a wonderful place, Matt. And I'll be working with children."

He was pleased.

"Matt?"

"Hmm?" His fingers slipped closer, the satin turning to velvet under his touch.

"I said . . . before . . . there were a couple of things . . ." A gasp of pleasure cut into whatever she was trying to say as he found her.

"Yes, sweet?" His own breathing was ragged as he discovered a hot, wet welcome.

"Something . . . we need . . . to get straight." Her eyes closed and she took short, quick breaths.

He slipped two fingers into the slick sheath. "And what's that, Jennifer?"

She forced her eyes open. "This compulsion of yours to make my decisions has to go."

"No problem, sweet. If you like, you can make all the decisions for both of us."

"That would certainly be a change. I can't imagine you giving up command."

"You sound like you don't believe I can do it." His fingers spread inside her, provoking a harsh gasp from her. "Let's give it a trial run, sweet. For your first decision, why don't you decide where."

"Where what?"

"Where we're going to make love, of course." Slowly, he withdrew his hand from between her thighs. "It's entirely up to you, Jennifer."

Her smile was sweetly smug as she lifted a hand and waggled it in the direction of the telephone. "I'm so glad you're going to be sensible about this," she said as he opened the drawer and searched inside until he discovered a pile of foil packets near the back.

He grabbed one and ripped it open.

She grinned. "Another thing, Colonel."

"The name's Matt, sweet."

"Well, Matt," she said in a silken voice as she slid off the counter and moved toward him, "don't you think it will be easier to put that on if you take your pants off first?"

"This decision making is already going to your head," he growled, sliding an arm around her waist. "But as long as you're in charge . . ."

His words faded into thin air as Jennifer did just that.

Take charge.

He couldn't imagine why he hadn't thought of it before.

Epilogue

Matt checked the array of instruments, then turned the flying of the Piper Cub over to Jennifer.

"But you *know* I don't know how to fly!" She cowered back in her seat, giving him a horrified glare.

He just grinned. "Nothing to it, sweet. We have a five-thousand-foot clearance below us and nothing above us but more air. Now just put your hands on the yoke and steer." He crossed his arms over his chest and stared out the windshield, sliding a glance to the instruments to ensure they were as he'd left them. They were, of course. He'd engaged the automatic pilot before pushing the yoke over to Jennifer.

She didn't know that, though.

When she hesitated, he gave her a chiding glance. "You're the one who decided she wanted to learn to fly. I'm just following through."

She crossed her eyes and gritted her teeth. "I assumed there would be a few preliminaries, Colonel. Like ground school, for one."

"You said you weren't sure you had the patience for ground school."

"*And you listened to me?*" In the tiny cabin, her voice rose to a near shriek.

"I always listen to you, Jennifer. I thought you knew that."

"I don't know what to do," she wailed, her glance rotating between him and the yoke in front of her.

"Put your hands on it, sweet. It won't bite."

She gingerly touched the yoke, her fingers finally sliding around it as though it were a lifeline she didn't quite trust. "I'll get you for this."

"I love your promises." He pointed to a dial that had a little airplane in the center. "Keep that plane level on the center line and you'll be fine."

"How?"

"You decide."

"I'm beginning to hate that word." She peered closely at the dial. Matt settled into his seat and stared at the woman he loved. His wife.

He still wasn't used to it. Marriage. Knowing that Jennifer was determined to spend the rest of her life loving him.

As he loved her.

Their honeymoon had been a spectacular success. A week loafing on the beaches of Tahiti followed by yet another week of the same. Matt had wanted to take her on to New Zealand, but she'd refused. There was time for everything, she'd said.

It wasn't as if they had to do it all at once. They had their whole lives in which to explore the world. New Zealand could wait for another time.

Besides, she hadn't finished decorating the living room yet.

Her sly smile of satisfaction interrupted his daydream. "That toy plane is exactly where it's supposed to be. Flying isn't so tough, Colonel."

He grinned. It was time to pay her back for nearly destroying his papa-san chair. "Think you've got the hang of it, Jennifer?"

She checked the dial again and nodded.

"See that switch over there?" he asked.

"What switch?"

"The one labeled 'automatic pilot.'"

She nodded again.

"Turn it off, sweet, and let's see what you can really do."

THE EDITOR'S CORNER

Next month LOVESWEPT presents an Easter parade of six fabulous romances. Not even April showers can douse the terrific mood you'll be in after reading each and every one of these treasures.

The hero of Susan Connell's new LOVESWEPT, #606, is truly **SOME KIND OF WONDERFUL.** As mysterious and exciting as the Greek islands he calls home, Alex Stoner is like a gorgeous god whose mouth promises pagan pleasures. He's also a cool businessman who never lets a woman get close. But prim and proper Sandy Patterson, widow of his college roommate, is unlike any he's ever known, and he sets out to make her ache for his own brand of passion. Susan takes you on a roller coaster of emotion with this romance.

Kay Hooper continues her MEN OF MYSTERIES PAST series with **HUNTING THE WOLFE,** LOVESWEPT #607. Security expert Wolfe Nickerson appeared in the first book in the series, **THE TOUCH OF MAX,** LOVESWEPT #595, and in this new novel, he almost finds himself bested by a pint-sized computer programmer. Storm Tremaine blows into his life like a force of nature, promising him the chase of his life . . . and hinting she's fast enough to catch him! When he surrenders to her womanly charms, he doesn't know that Storm holds a secret . . . a secret that could forever destroy his trust. Kay is at her best with this terrific love story.

BREATHLESS, LOVESWEPT #608 by Diane Pershing, is how Hollis Blake feels when Tony Stellini walks into her gift shop. The tall, dark, and sensuous lawyer makes the air sizzle with his wildfire energy, and for the first time Hollis longs to taste every pleasure she's never had, pursue all the dreams she's been denied. Her innocence stirs an overpowering desire in Tony, but he senses that with this untouched beauty, he has to take it one slow, delicious step at a time. This is a romance to relish, a treat from Diane.

Linda Cajio begins **DANCING IN THE DARK,** LOVESWEPT #609, with an eye-opening scene in which the hero is engaged in a sacred ceremony and dancing naked in the woods! Jake Halford feels a little silly performing the men's movement ritual, but Charity Brown feels downright embarrassed at catching him at it. How can she ever work with her company's new vice president without remembering the thrilling sight of his muscles and power? The way Linda has these two learning how to mix business and pleasure is a pure delight.

HANNAH'S HUNK, LOVESWEPT #610 by Sandra Chastain, is nothing less than a sexy rebel with a southern drawl . . . and an ex-con whom Hannah Clendening "kidnaps" so he could pose for the cover of her Fantasy Romance. Dan Bailey agrees, but only if Hannah plays the heroine and he gets to kiss her. When desire flares between them like a force field, neither believes that what they feel could last. Of course Sandra, with her usual wit and charm, makes sure there's a happily ever after for this unusual couple.

Finally, there's **THE TROUBLE WITH MAGIC,** LOVESWEPT #611 by Mary Kay McComas. Harriet Wheaton has an outrageous plan to keep Payton Dunsmore from foreclosing on the great manor house on Jovette Island. Marooning them there, she tells him that she's trying to fulfill the old legend of enemies meeting on Jovette and falling in love! Payton's furious at first, but he soon succumbs to the enchantment of the island . . . and Harriet herself. Mary Kay delivers pure magic with this marvelous romance.

On sale this month from FANFARE are four outstanding novels. If you missed **TEMPERATURES RISING** by blockbuster author Sandra Brown when it first came out, now's your chance to grab a copy of this wonderfully evocative love story. Chantal duPont tells herself that she needs Scout Ritland only to build a much-needed bridge on the South Pacific island she calls home. And when the time comes for him to leave, she must make the painful decision of letting him go—or risking everything by taking a chance on love.

From beloved author Rosanne Bittner comes **OUTLAW HEARTS,** a stirring new novel of heart-stopping danger and burning desire. At twenty, Miranda Hayes has known more than her share of heartache and loss. Then she clashes with the notorious gunslinger Jake Harkner, a hard-hearted loner with a price on his head, and finds within herself a deep well of courage . . . and feelings of desire she's never known before.

Fanfare is proud to publish **THE LAST HIGHWAYMAN,** the first historical romance by Katherine O'Neal, a truly exciting new voice in women's fiction. In this delectable action-packed novel, Christina has money, power, and position, but she has never known reckless passion, never found enduring love . . . until she is kidnapped by a dangerously handsome bandit who needs her to heal his tormented soul.

In the bestselling tradition of Danielle Steel, **CONFI-DENCES** by Penny Hayden is a warm, deeply moving novel about four "thirty-something" mothers whose lives are interwoven by a long-held secret—a secret that could now save the life of a seventeen-year-old boy dying of leukemia.

Also available now in the hardcover edition from Double-day is **MASK OF NIGHT** by Lois Wolfe, a stunning historical novel of romantic suspense. When an actress and a cattle rancher join forces against a diabolical villain, the result is an unforgettable story of love and vengeance.

Happy reading!

With warmest wishes,

Nita Taublib

Nita Taublib
Associate Publisher
LOVESWEPT and FANFARE

OFFICIAL RULES TO WINNERS CLASSIC SWEEPSTAKES

No Purchase necessary. To enter the sweepstakes follow instructions found elsewhere in this offer. You can also enter the sweepstakes by hand printing your name, address, city, state and zip code on a 3" x 5" piece of paper and mailing it to: Winners Classic Sweepstakes, P.O. Box 785, Gibbstown, NJ 08027. Mail each entry separately. Sweepstakes begins 12/1/91. Entries must be received by 6/1/93. Some presentations of this sweepstakes may feature a deadline for the Early Bird prize. If the offer you receive does, then to be eligible for the Early Bird prize your entry must be received according to the Early Bird date specified. Not responsible for lost, late, damaged, misdirected, illegible or postage due mail. Mechanically reproduced entries are not eligible. All entries become property of the sponsor and will not be returned.

Prize Selection/Validations: Winners will be selected in random drawings on or about 7/30/93, by VENTURA ASSOCIATES, INC., an independent judging organization whose decisions are final. Odds of winning are determined by total number of entries received. Circulation of this sweepstakes is estimated not to exceed 200 million. Entrants need not be present to win. All prizes are guaranteed to be awarded and delivered to winners. Winners will be notified by mail and may be required to complete an affidavit of eligibility and release of liability which must be returned within 14 days of date of notification or alternate winners will be selected. Any guest of a trip winner will also be required to execute a release of liability. Any prize notification letter or any prize returned to a participating sponsor, Bantam Doubleday Dell Publishing Group, Inc., its participating divisions or subsidiaries, or VENTURA ASSOCIATES, INC. as undeliverable will be awarded to an alternate winner. Prizes are not transferable. No multiple prize winners except as may be necessary due to unavailability, in which case a prize of equal or greater value will be awarded. Prizes will be awarded approximately 90 days after the drawing. All taxes, automobile license and registration fees, if applicable, are the sole responsibility of the winners. Entry constitutes permission (except where prohibited) to use winners' names and likenesses for publicity purposes without further or other compensation.

Participation: This sweepstakes is open to residents of the United States and Canada, except for the province of Quebec. This sweepstakes is sponsored by Bantam Doubleday Dell Publishing Group, Inc. (BDD), 666 Fifth Avenue, New York, NY 10103. Versions of this sweepstakes with different graphics will be offered in conjunction with various solicitations or promotions by different subsidiaries and divisions of BDD. Employees and their families of BDD, its division, subsidiaries, advertising agencies, and VENTURA ASSOCIATES, INC., are not eligible.

Canadian residents, in order to win, must first correctly answer a time limited arithmetical skill testing question. Void in Quebec and wherever prohibited or restricted by law. Subject to all federal, state, local and provincial laws and regulations.

Prizes: The following values for prizes are determined by the manufacturers' suggested retail prices or by what these items are currently known to be selling for at the time this offer was published. Approximate retail values include handling and delivery of prizes. Estimated maximum retail value of prizes: 1 Grand Prize ($27,500 if merchandise or $25,000 Cash); 1 First Prize ($3,000); 5 Second Prizes ($400 each); 35 Third Prizes ($100 each); 1,000 Fourth Prizes ($9.00 each) ; 1 Early Bird Prize ($5,000); Total approximate maximum retail value is $50,000. Winners will have the option of selecting any prize offered at level won. Automobile winner must have a valid driver's license at the time the car is awarded. Trips are subject to space and departure availability. Certain black-out dates may apply. Travel must be completed within one year from the time the prize is awarded. Minors must be accompanied by an adult. Prizes won by minors will be awarded in the name of parent or legal guardian.

For a list of Major Prize Winners (available after 7/30/93): send a self-addressed, stamped envelope entirely separate from your entry to: Winners Classic Sweepstakes Winners, P.O. Box 825, Gibbstown, NJ 08027. Requests must be received by 6/1/93. DO NOT SEND ANY OTHER CORRESPONDENCE TO THIS P.O. BOX.